BELINDA
or
The Rivals

by
A.S.H.

Anansi Toronto

Foreword, copyright © James Polk, 1975.

Cover design by Ian Leventhal.

Published with the assistance of the Canada Council and the Ontario Arts Council by

The House of Anansi Press Limited
35 Britain Street
Toronto, Canada

ISBN: 0-88784-333-6   Found Books 2

Canadian Shared Cataloguing in Publication Data

    Holmes, Abraham S., 19th cent.
      Belinda, or, The rivals / by A.S.H. —
(Found books; 2)

    First published in 1843 by Bagg and Harmon, Detroit.
    Also published in a limited ed. in 1970 by the Alcuin Society, Vancouver.
    ISBN 0-88784-333-6 pa.

    I. Title.   II. Title: The rivals.

    PS8415.O   C813.'3
    PR9199.2.H

FOREWORD

"A.S.H.", the author of *Belinda*, has been identified with fair certainty as Abraham S. Holmes, a law student, journalist, and the son of a Methodist minister living in the Chatham area of Kent County, Ontario. His tale of "the Canadian coquette" was published in 1843 by Bagg and Harmon, the proprietors of the Detroit *Free Press*, and almost all copies of the first edition have disappeared. It may be that Holmes's neighbours disliked seeing themselves and their community caricatured and quietly got rid of as many *Belinda*s as they could; perhaps Holmes himself, or his father, had second thoughts. Whatever happened, only a single copy survives, in the Burton Historical Collection of the Detroit Public Library, although in 1970 the Alcuin Society brought out a numbered edition, with an introduction by Carl F. Klinck, limited to 450 copies. Yet *Belinda* deserves wider circulation, for it is a readable, literate and often quite funny novel — and certainly an unexpected book to come out of what was then the Canadian frontier.

Belinda is, first of all, a spoof of the sentimental novel of seduction, a variety of popular fiction which had grown up in the shadow of Samuel Richardson's *Pamela* and *Clarissa*. In Holmes's time, such bestsellers as *The Power of Sympathy* and *Charlotte Temple* were feeding an insatiable public taste for pious morality and sexual titillation, and he is mocking the conventions of the form with his characters' feverish emotions, their penchant for letter-writing, his own insistence that this outrageous book is "a tale of real life". The plot formula for this kind of novel varied, but usually a sensitive young maiden, despite moral scruples and religious upbringing, finds herself seduced ("ruined") by a member of the upper classes. Pregnant, despised by family and friends, she gives way to much fainting, repentance, hysteria, and wandering in the snow; then she has her child and dies at great length, forgiving everybody and apparently forgiven by Heaven for all her troubles. Holmes follows the pattern, but he switches the sexual roles: Belinda is the seducer, and the men declare themselves ruined.

So when Fitz Rowland is spurned by the lady, he rushes off into the wilderness like any sentimental heroine, to contemplate suicide and weep and rant in the approved style. This particular swain comes to his senses soon enough, for Belinda is not a destroyer. She is frankly out for sex, conquest and a good time, and seems indifferent to the race or social rank of the available men, trying out Scotsman and Jew, shepherd and squire, with true democratic zeal. Although Holmes must condemn her postures of feminine gentility and inconstant heart, she is a likeable rake, and even after the arrival of her child, little Ichabod, a mere six weeks after marriage, her startled husband is quickly charmed into forgiving this error of timing. Belinda almost gets away with it, but Holmes cannot resist burlesquing the required deathbed scene, and so, with much high-flown language, his heroine graciously accepts eternity and a moist-eyed funeral, with the surrounding countryside as upset "as if some patriot hero, the pillar and support of his country, had fallen."

Holmes was by no means the first writer to poke fun at sentimental fiction, and his control of the parody and the pacing is sometimes uncertain. But *Belinda* goes beyond literary send-up, for Holmes based his fiction, however obliquely, on real characters and events in Kent County, and the book gives us a valuable glimpse into a small Ontario community of the 1840's. Of course the provincial setting is part of the joke, for no matter how poetically desperate the characters become, small-town manners and Ontario common sense are always there in the background. Still, the visits, the church going, some of the conversations and landscapes, the professions of the men, and the very sophistication of Holmes's writing suggest that life in a pioneering village in Canada West was more civilized than we might imagine. Belinda's circle is an educated one, although the author is quick to mock its pretensions to refinement: Belinda may know Byron and *Don Quixote*, but she also misquotes Shakespeare ("There is a destiny which slopes our ends") and likes to play the accordian before bedtime.

Holmes might have gone on to write better novels, perhaps in the manner of Sara Jeanette Duncan's *The Imperialist*, but he apparently gave it up, and his one frivolous book was not a major event in the development of Canadian literature. But if *Belinda* is not as essential as, say, *Wacousta* or Mrs. Moodie, it can remind us that life in pre-Confederation Canada was not solely devoted to roughing it in the bush and that all our fictional characters are not thin-lipped, melancholy and victimized. Belinda, with her cheerful sexuality and wayward schemes may be the exception which proves the rule, but it is good to remember that she was possible.

James Polk
Toronto

Note: The text for this edition of *Belinda* is taken from the surviving copy in the Burton Historical Collection in the Detroit Public Library, and we thank the Library for its assistance. A few typographical errors and misspellings have been corrected, but the punctuation, grammar, and nearly all of the spellings from the original edition have been preserved. For further background on the novel, see Carl F. Klinck's introduction to the Alcuin edition (1970), Fred C. Hamil's article in *Ontario History* (volume 39, 1947), and Marilyn Davis's excellent study in *Journal of Canadian Fiction* (volume 2, summer, 1973).

ADVERTISEMENT

The following true narrative is offered to the reading public as the first production of its author, without any very sanguine hopes on his part of its being accepted. He is very sensible of his unripeness for authorship; considering the high degree of perfection to which English composition and the art of pleasing, have been carried by late writers. The reader may presume that he finds much discrepancy in the scheme; many improbabilities and inconsistencies, which show a want of invention, or of judgment, or of acquaintance with human nature. To this it might be replied, that as nothing but truth has been intentionally given a place, there was no scheme formed, and where there was no plan, there was consequently no room for invention. As to *human nature*, it is indeed to be hoped that there are not many among our species, whose natures have any thing in them agreeable to some circumstances which have been unwillingly related.

The public's most obedient,
Most humble servant,
THE AUTHOR.

CHAPTER 1.

In heaven and in earth, the grand principle of action is love. It pervades every soul of every class of intelligencies; operates upon and connects objects at inconceivable distances; and, like the caloric of universal nature, warms and enlivens all sentient beings with its invigorating influence. Were it not for the latent fire which all matter contains, the very air we breathe would congeal into a solid mass, and were it not for love we ourselves would be no better than mere inanimate clods. But, alas! like all other passions, this (which we share in common with the Deity himself,) has, by the inhabitants of our perverse planet, been very greatly abused, warped, in many cases, from its original use; and made the occasion of death rather than of life.

If we may believe the legends of former times, it was, a few centuries ago, not thought very mysterious or inexplicable for a lady to faint or even to die for love. It was not thought particularly worthy of note when two or more gentlemen strove with each other for the upper place in some fair one's affections. In the days of chivalry, it was nothing strange or uncommon for Knights errant to quarrel about the possession of a heart; to challenge to single combat; and at last to enter the lists and settle the dispute in the most gallant style.

But a very great change has taken place in society. A rapid movement has been made. Whether we have improved upon the wisdom of our ancestors and advanced in the scale of beings; or whether the march has been a retrograde one, I shall not pretend to determine. One thing is certain, that mighty revolutions have taken place in the world, not only in the civil constitutions of the nations, or in the religious establishments of different countries, but in the manners and customs of the people generally. And in nothing have greater changes been effected than in our notions of the tender passion.

Formerly, courtship appears to have been the principal business of a certain stage in life; now, we give it but little part of our time or thoughts. Formerly, wooing was reduced to an art, and studied with the same attention as that of cultivating the earth; of navigating the ocean; or of war — neither flattery nor detraction, stratagem nor open force, was neglected: now, men, it would almost seem, have agreed to leave the thing to fate — perhaps I ought to say to Providence — and remain quite inactive until, between two, a mutual affection takes place, which, with a power like that of gravitation, will gradually but surely draw them together, and consolidate them into one.

Formerly, a suitor endeavored to recommend himself to his mistress, by convincing her that he, by his own prowess, was able to protect her from the approaches of his rivals; now, we would purchase esteem and love by merely *pretending* that we do deserve, and, (with a proviso,) will return them.

Indeed, we have gone so far in controlling our natures by a frigid philosophy, that we hear some even express their doubts whether love ever did act as an irresistible impulse, and constrain man, "like the prowling wolf all night to wake," or woman, like Queen Dido at the loss of her lover, to plunge the dagger into her own breast.

But the tale which I am about to relate satisfactorily proves that nothing of this kind, how improbable soever it may be, is too wonderful to be true; that stories of love, mixed with murder, sometimes deserve our credence; and that when the passion gains full sway over the mind and operates with all its force, it is (if the expression will be pardoned me) nothing less than a species of insanity. I am not yet, however, quite persuaded to subscribe the declaration of the great Virgil, when he says that, in men and brutes, "love is lord of all and is in all the *same*."

My tale I must confess, though I am fully prepared to vouch for its authenticity, will savor very much of a romance or a novel. That influence so goddess-like should be exerted by any human being, is almost too much for belief. That the scene should be so often changed and always with some additional circumstances to excite our wonder and astonishment, makes it look like the invention of some more than ordinarily prolific imagination. And yet it shall be merely a plain statement of facts — merely a record of events which have transpired in our own country, during our own recollection; and have come under our own observation.

CHAPTER II.

Miss Belinda Howard was a young lady of uncommon personal beauty and of many accomplishments, both natural and acquired.

She was the pride of her parents and the brightest ornament of the circle in which she moved. Her education was solid as well as ornamental; her manners were easy and unaffected; her conversation animated and interesting; her air modest and unassuming. And above all, she possessed a calm, unruffled mind — always willing to forgive, and presuming upon the charitable judgment of others in return. The future, to her imagination, was all one unclouded day — one continued sunshine, where pleasures would succeed pleasures in unbroken succession forever.

They who are possessed of such a temper, may consider themselves as peculiarly favored. A person of an habitually cheerful frame, feels but half the miseries of sickness, poverty, or any other misfortune; while one of those unthankful, cross-grained, six-elbowed creatures, to whose vitiated fancy good is always evil and order always disarrangement, not only doubles the effect of real accident and creates ideal ones, but adulterates the pleasures of health, plenty, and every other blessing with an unfortunate and ungrateful disposition.

Belinda's father, J. Howard, Esq., was a wealthy landholder in the county of Kent, in Canada. He was a gentleman of high standing in society — a man of enlarged views and a liberal mind — courteous and hospitable to strangers — a tender parent and a worthy citizen. Belinda being his eldest daughter, and nature having done much for her, he resolved to give her every other advantage, that she might not only equal, but eclipse the first and finest ladies in the place. No expense was spared to store her mind with useful knowledge, or decorate her person with the refinements of art and fashion.

As might be expected, she had many *admirers* among the opposite sex, as well as many among her own, who *envied* her for her cultivated genius, the attractions of her face, and the symmetry of her form. All who knew her were either the warmest friends or the most vindictive foes. And, to judge of her conduct and character by this criterion, one would perhaps be apt to infer that she unfortunately had not hit the proper mean betwixt the two extremes of coquetry on the one hand and prudery on the other; the former of which is despicable enough, but the latter is a libel upon the nature and name of woman. At the time of which I now speak, however, she appears not to have been a finished character of either class. Her eyes never roved with perfect boldness on the faces of men, neither was she unnecessarily coy. She possessed a great facility in changing her external appearance and conversation to suit the temper of the company in which she happened to fall. Among the good, she was the most religious person in the world — among the bad, her principles were dubious. She was better acquainted with the bible, and had read more novels — could talk more like a divine, and tell more of what had never transpired — could pray more fervently, and dance more elegantly, than any other female of her age I ever knew.

She was soon besieged by suitors, among whom Mac—, a Scotchman, and Barnabas, a young Jew, were conspicuous; and, for a while, it might be said,

"Favors to none, to all she smiles extends;
Oft she rejects, but never once offends."

Her plan appears to have been to let none despair, but conciliate all; "to be all things to all men, that by all means she might gain some."

The importunities of Mack were answered ambiguously, — if the language of the young Jew, (Mr. B.) was too plain for an equivocal reply, she would squeeze his hand, then blush and "look inexpressible things." If he still urged her to give him an explicit and categorical answer, she was not yet driven to her last resource, but was always ready with some device, without speaking a word, (and yet she had a tongue,) to make him believe that she had tacitly consented. A regular court was established, where she sat, like a queen on her throne, receiving and answering petitions; dispensing rewards, and sending into banishment, as might suit her own most gracious pleasure. Those who had favors to ask, were admitted to private audience at proper and improper hours; no particular etiquette was necessary to be observed; no particular class of persons was excluded — the shoemaker, the merchant, and the gentleman, met with an equally flattering reception. Her expressions of respect and esteem were unbounded; her speech, upon general topics, was engaging; but her replies to close interrogations, were as obscure and indefinite as those of an oracle.

The young Jew, willing to terminate a negotiation which had been long pending, to the destruction of his own peace and exposing him to the enmity of the high-mettled Mack; and anxious to know the issue of his hopes, addressed the following letter to the fair Belinda. It was dated,

"*The Shores of the Great Lake*,
September 15th, 1832.

"My Dearest Belinda — That *I love you* truly, sincerely, passionately, and will eternally, I am sure you are convinced. I do not, however, suppose you to be so ignorant of men, in general, as to imagine that my having told you this a hundred and a hundred times in our tete-a-tete conversations, or now writing it in italic characters, can possibly pass with you for demonstration.

"But there is a better and safer criterion by which to judge — a something which I believe poetry itself has failed fully to express in language. It can be heard in the tone of voice — seen in every gesture and motion — perceived in the eye, and felt in the pulse. This I hope your discerning mind has not failed to discover, and to mark as a broad line of distinction between myself and Mack. You are satisfied, then, that you have my heart, and I (pardon me for saying so,) almost believe that I have yours.

"Will you not, sweetheart, declare a mutual affection? And if our love be reciprocal, our fates and fortunes now are one; and shall we not enter into a vow before God and a select company of our friends, that our two *selves* shall become one, and remain such "so long as we both shall live?"

"Please write me as soon as convenient, with a positive answer of 'yes' or 'no,' to this last question.

"With sincere wishes for your welfare,

"I remain your constant lover,
"S.B."

When this letter was handed her by her little brother, who had brought it from the post office, Belinda was walking in the garden with Mack, and, although she endeavored to conceal it, his quick eye fell upon the address, and he instantly suspected the young Jew's hand. This was sufficient to arouse him. His worst fears he now imagined realized. He recollected many circumstances of which he thought nothing at the time. She had, upon a certain occasion, given the Jew a more hearty shake of the hand, than mere friendship would have induced; in company their eyes met each other more frequently than they could have done by chance; and, indeed, he had been known to stop at her father's oftener than his business could have called him there. And trifles light as air, Shakspeare says, are to the green eyed monster, jealousy, "confirmation strong as proof from holy writ." Mack inquired what paper that was she just received? She answered "it was nothing but yesterday's journal, which you have seen." "No," says Mack, with an expression upon his countenance peculiar to himself — half smile half scowl, "I saw it and read the address." "O, well," says she, laughing, "I only wished to try you — to see whether you do actually love me as you profess to; but do not be so suspicious, it is from a *female* friend of mine in town." With this Mack expressed himself perfectly satisfied; still, however, begging the privilege of opening and reading it for her. This, his love declined, by saying that the writer was one with whom she had never wished to hold a correspondence — an ignorant and foolish girl, incapable of writing a decent letter, and that her clever Scotchman should not do her the honor of reading it. Convinced that neither praying nor parleying would avail him, he threw his brawny arm around her slender waist, planted a kiss or two upon her cheek, and playfully wrested it from her. Belinda struggled and entreated, but to no purpose; Mack was determined to know who this *female friend* was.

The contents of the letter, as well as its author, were soon known, and as Mack hurriedly ran it over, the pale and red shades chased each other across his face like waves of the beautiful expanse of water before them. Belinda was full of expressions of surprise and astonishment, that she could have been so deceived in the hand writing on the back of the letter; and above all, that the *impudent puppy*, to whom she had scarcely spoken more than once or twice in her life, and who even then had not dared so much as to hint at any thing relating to courtship, should presume to write her a letter of that description! "But," replies Mack, still gazing at the unfortunate paper which he held in his hand, "this is a very mysterious letter! There is one thing here, which still sticks in my throat; I cannot force it down. You, my own Belinda, have affirmed that you have scarcely spoken with Barnabas, and never upon nice subjects, and yet he says here that he has a *hundred times, in tete-a-tete conversations, told you that he loved you!*"

"I am extremely surprised at his boldness and at his duplicity. He is getting above himself. He expects attentions, and claims privileges to which his rank in society, and moral worth do not entitle him."

"That the vagabond is most audaciously false, as well as a consummate villain, I am very ready to admit, but the devil himself never tells a lie unless it be to serve some end. Now the Jew must have very well known that, if what he says were untrue, you could in a moment detect it; and that it could not possibly recommend him to your notice to say that he had told you to your face, something about which he had never spoken a word. We will leave these knots, which, perhaps, time will untie, and examine the other parts of the letter. In his whole yarn, the rough clown had not once told you that you were pretty. Is this, my angel, to be endured? You, who are the paragon of women — whose face expresses the perfection of beauty, whose form is dignity, and whose 'neck is like the tower of David, and head like Mount Carmel,' to receive so cold, calculating, business-style kind of a letter?

"Upon my word, Belinda, I never saw in all my life a creature half so fair! Never was a woman adored as you are; my happiness — nay, my very being depends upon the fiat of a word breathed from between your velvet lips, say once more that you love me, and that you will be mine!"

"My dear Mack," exclaimed Belinda, (as if she had just waked from a trance,) "what shall we do with this wretched scrawl? shall we send it back to the rustic who wrote it, or will you assist me in composing a reply which will shut his vulgar mouth, and quench the fire of his love?" To this latter proposal Mack in a moment consented. A letter (which was never sent, and which I shall not transcribe on account of the extreme rudeness and indecency of the language used,) was soon dictated by the horned Scotchman, written by herself, and sealed with her own seal. With a stream of senseless and bombastic flattery, with a kiss and a promise, but, at the same time, with a fallen countenance like that of Cain when his offering was not respected, Mack took his leave.

Miss Howard retired to her room, spent a turning of the hour-glass with Mr. S., wrote a letter to Barnabas, took up lord Byron's poems, sung one of Wesley's hymns, read a page or two in Don Quixotte, and a chapter in the New Testament, played Yankee Doodle upon her accordian, knelt down and prayed for the spread of gospel truth and knowledge in every part of the world, for success in all her enterprises, protection through the night, a long and agreeable life, an easy transit, and a happy eternity — undressed and went to bed. The next morning, Belinda handed Mack the following letter, which he, supposing it to be the one endited by himself, forwarded to the young Jew:

"Clifton Hall, Sept. 20th, 1832."

"Dear Sir — I am in receipt of your favor of the 15th, and for the assurances of continued love which it contains, I sincerely thank you.

"Neither to your person nor character have I any particular objections; indeed, you are the only person for whom I ever felt that attachment which I think they who form connections 'according to God's holy ordinance,' ought always to feel.

"I believe you love me because you tell me so; and this is more than I can say of any other young gentleman, having never heard such professions from any but yourself.

"Please write me often; it is the greatest pleasure of

my life to read your beautiful letters.

Yours, very sincerely,
"Belinda."

"To Mr. — Barnabas.

"P.S. I forgot your last question until I had closed my letter, and it would certainly look awkward and displaced to see a thing of such importance in postscript. I therefore beg that you will kindly pardon me.

"B.H."

When Mr. Barnabas received Miss Howard's epistle, knowing in a moment from whom it came, the blood rushed through every vein and artery of his body towards the seat of life as if to congratulate him. His heart fluttered and was unsteady; for a moment all motion would appear to cease, as if in dread that a dagger more keen than ever steel was made, was about to be driven home, then again flushed with hope, it would play with redoubled fury. The young Jew took out his pen knife, carefully opening the letter without breaking the seal, for the name of "Belinda" was upon it, and, as he read, thus noted those parts which he thought most remarkable.

"Dear Sir." I had rather, much rather, see my name in the place of *sir*. That is a very common way of commencing a note upon business, or to one about whose love or hatred we feel quite indifferent. She has no *particular* objections to me — this sounds as if there were some thing, how small soever, in the way. If the dear creature loved me as I do her, she'd have no objections at all. *Attachment* — the overflowing of love is but coldly expressed by this word. Why, I have an *attachment* for my brothers, for my species, for my home, for my country, but I love them not as I do thee, thou ever fleeting object of desire. She *knows nothing of man by experience!* I hope not, and yet if I were sane — I'm not beside myself! no, I hope she does not. She believes that I love her because I tell her so — and must I wait until she tell me the

same before it is believed? She does not deign so much as to style herself *my lover* at the close!

"The question is evaded — forgotten! that is worse. Well, I am like a feather in the air, still hang between two opposite currents, and make no progress. If I could live without her, another effort, nor pen nor tongue, should ever make. But this is impossible. Then come the worst! 'Tis death or victory.'"

It was some weeks after these transactions, that Mack and Barnabas happened to meet at a hotel near the Clifton Hall. They had been old friends, and the Jew was exceedingly happy at meeting — made many inquiries concerning the people of the neighborhood, and at last about the family of Esq. Howard. Mack knew nothing of the Esquire or his family! *(Going.)*

"Were I not a tee-totaller, Mack, wine should be brought. I'd drink your health and you should mine before you go."

"Try me with a glass of cold water, and I will not drink the health of the wretch who, with fair outside, has, in a clandestine way, endeavored to injure me."

"To injure you! that cannot be. I labor to advance my own interests, by attending to my own affairs; besides, my place of residence lies so distant, and my occupation is so different from yours, as to render it impossible for our interests to clash, or the objects of our pursuit to be the same."

"The object of our pursuit, villain, is the same."

"Then let us accommodate the matter — how the same?"

"What brought you here to-day? It was to see the fair Belinda. I shall be uncompromising. If you wish to re-establish peace, you must evacuate the ground you are on; relinquish all your vain pretensions, and, ere the shadow upon the dial plate move one inch, turn your horse's head toward home."

"Oh, I now perceive the cause of your ill humor," says Barnabas sneeringly, "and confess, moreover, your surmisings are correct. But speak not quite so boastingly; I am not easily frightened. The fair one whose name you have profaned by mentioning, I'll visit if I live, this night."

"'Tis at your peril you persist." *(Exit.)*

Whether the young Jew considered his former successes with Miss Howard, the letter he had received, or the determined pugnacity of Mack, his fate appeared in a very questionable shape. He, however, resolved at all hazards to make one desperate attempt to see her, and, if this should fail, to leave forever his native land. He did so — met Mack in the yard, and, unwilling to soil his hands upon the Buckskin, spurned him with his foot away. What sort of a reception Belinda gave him, is unknown; one thing is certain, that, in that section of the country, the noble but much-injured Barnabas was never heard of after!

The *intimacy* between the Scotchman and Miss Howard was now still more perceivable. It was even hinted that this word should be taken in its most infamous sense. Mrs. Howard, Belinda's mother, an amiable and good woman — though unwilling to believe harm even of strangers, upon the testimony of every idle tattler, much less of her own daughter — was harrassed beyond endurance by these ridiculous rumors. Her pious heart, which had been so often gratified by the religious disposition and, as she imagined, suitable conduct and upright intentions of Belinda, was pained when she was made the subject of remarks and coarse jests. She (Mrs. H.) consequently determined, with the concurrence of her husband, upon sending her, for a few months, from home. This, as their circumstances were easy, they were enabled to do, in such a manner as that she should appear respectable wherever she went.

Belinda was transported with the idea of traveling as soon as the plan was suggested to her. She very well knew what attractions she possessed, how quickly her pretty face would recommend her to men of gallantry; and her fascinating manners chain them to her chariot wheels. She gave Mack every assurance that he should never be forgotten, she was only going to take a trip for pleasure, to visit her kind aunt in the west, and would return before midsummer. Every thing was arranged for the journey, and as the carriage whirled her from the scene of many enjoyments and rattled over the graveled walks which led from the Clifton Hall, the deluged eyes, as well as the waiving of handkerchiefs, showed that the beautiful, the young, the lovely Belinda still had friends.

Perhaps I would be pardonable in noticing the lines handed her by Mack, who accompanied her a few miles on her way, poured his whole soul into her ears, and endeavored to impress upon her mind the justness of his claims. She bowed to everything he said, and acknowledged the equity of his suit; but like some distinguished statesman, she was particularly careful just then not to explain herself too far.

The Scotchman's poetical effusion commenced with a verse from Lord Byron.

"Maid of —, ere we part,
Give, Oh! give me back my heart,
Or, since that's by thee possessed,
Keep it now and take the rest."

I'm like a vessel on the sea,
With masts and rigging blown away,
Without a pilot or a boat,
As winds and tides change I must float.

I've heard that lotteries were lies,
I bought a ticket, drew a prize,
But it is plain I gave too much,
For, what is mine I dare not touch.

Take these gloves, accept this ring,
In mournful tune my verses sing,
And when you're far away, alack!
Think, fair Belinda, of poor Mack.

The small present was accepted, as a matter of course, and Belinda, with her usual celerity and habitually religious vein, returned the following impromptu, written upon a slip of paper with her pencil:

Both experience and information,
   Teach *us* to beware and take heed,
To suspect every man in the nation,
   Of whatever name, tongue, color, or creed.
One fiend 'mong twelve saints I believe,
   Is the smallest proportion yet found;
It was this, where the chance to deceive,
   Was the least, and the preaching most sound;
How will *I* then trust others, brave Mack,
And on you whom I know, turn my back?
To Him whom I serve I now fervently pray,
That He'll bless you and me on some fair future day.

                                      BELINDA.

As no incident, uncommon to a lady traveling alone on a route where many different means of conveyance must be resorted to, occurred until after her arrival at her uncle's, we shall not follow her through her journey. It will be sufficient to say that whether in a private carriage, the stage coach, or on board the steamer, with her bible in her hand, which she always held sacred, she maintained the same serenity and composure, and was as easy of access as when she sat in her own room at the Clifton Hall.

CHAPTER III.

Every body knows that there is not in all these provinces an edifice which might properly be called a castle. But as strict propriety of language is not always consulted, things often take names to which they are not entitled. Thus, the house of Belinda's uncle, from its imposing structure and antique appearance, was called THE CASTLE; and he, perhaps from his manners and dimensions, *the old Burgher*. These convenient appellations being furnished to my hand, I shall make use of them without any further explanation or apology. The Castle stood upon a gentle declivity, in the midst of one of the most beautiful and fertile valleys in the world — hence sometimes called "the garden of British America." The Thames, a noble river, found its winding way, shaded by the willows which hanged from its banks, and ploughed by the numerous craft which were entrusted with her wealth, about a furlong from the Burgher's door. Through an opening in the wood a distant plain, speckled with thousands of cattle and horses grazing, was full in view. The respectable character of the neighborhood, the peaceable and accommodating disposition of the people, and its distance from the bustling city, all combined to make it a place to which Charles fifth of Germany himself, might have retired with pleasure.

Half a century ago, this delightful valley was all one dense wilderness. The walnut and the oak have left their enduring stumps in the earth to evidence their former majesty; a solitary wild deer may yet be seen bounding across the fields, followed by his deadly foe, the wolf; but the tens of thousands of aborigines, where are they? Why, their bones enrich the soil which we occupy — their dead carcases lie scattered up and down, and we, like so many cannibals, are eating them whenever we partake of any thing prepared from our boasted wheat and corn.

The old Burgher was one of those iron men, who neither experience themselves, nor believe any thing of tender feelings. A heart touched with pity, a tear of sympathy, the soft influences of love, were to him unintelligible gibberish, without sense or meaning His wife was a person of a very different temperament. She was never in her proper element unless something in which her tongue could engage was in agitation. Whether love between the young, or hatred between the old, it was a matter of total indifference to her. But her tongue! her tongue! I feel as if I could vent my spleen against the tongue of the shrew and busy body, of the clamorous and capricious combined, of her who, while

"She uses her husband like a fool,
And combs his head with a three legged stool,"

attends to nothing in her own house, but to everything in those of her neighbors', of her whose only business is to hear or tell some new thing; but for fear it might be thought that I was claiming a privilege which I was unwilling to allow the ladies themselves, I repress my honest indignation to proceed with something more pleasing to my reader, and more analogous to my own inclination and feelings.

It was Saturday evening, a few days after Belinda's arrival at the Castle, as she stood before her glass, under which, upon a stand,

"Together lay her prayer book and her paint,
At once to improve the sinner and the saint,"

that her aunt came to her room and asked her to walk. Perhaps I ought to say that between Belinda and her aunt, there was no consanguineous connection. The sun was just setting as they started on their first stroll together along the green, sloping banks of the meandering Thames.

Belinda would have been entertained at this time with remarks upon the beautiful fields of green wheat; the opening of the buds so early as the first of April; the immense herds of cattle returning from pasture; or the countless numbers of water fowl resting upon the bosom of the river; the like of which, at that season of the year, she had never been accustomed to see.

But the imagination or fancy of her aunt dwelt not with equal fondness upon the beauties of nature. Her intention was, to give Miss Howard a complete history of the inhabitants. The first of whom she spoke was a German, by the name of Van Corts; his youngest son, and heir to the estate on which he lived, unmarried — a young gentleman of uncommon sprightliness and great promise. "For him you must consider what nets to spread, what subtle baits to lay. Tomorrow you shall see him at church, and, although I would, by no means, have you neglect your devotions, you must now and then turn your eyes askance and give him a look which he can understand.

"In yon ancient looking pile, peering over the fruit trees by which it is surrounded, lives a widow lady of great respectability. Her husband died many years ago, universally lamented. He was a clergyman of Irish extraction, and to his preaching, but more to his living — to his precept, but more to his example — are principally to be attributed the superior civilization, and knowledge of religious subjects, of the people of this and contiguous settlements, over those of other parts of the country. There is one marriageable son, the eldest of a large family, among whom reign the most complete unison and perfect harmony. Now, although I prize myself as a peacemaker, I am actually sick and tired to death with the sameness of the friendship existing between these two families. I could almost consent, if it were in my power, to make war for the conscious pleasure and inward satisfaction of again bringing about, (to myself, at least,) an honorable peace!

"The Rev. Fitz Rowland, for that was the clergyman's name, labored not for popularity, and yet his posthumous reputation is incredible, and to form a connexion with his son would be no dishonorable alliance. Him I hope you will also see to-morrow. And to assist you in aiming Cupid's invisible darts, it might be observed that he is, though a person of moral worth, yet somewhat eccentric. Thoughtful and studious, it is difficult to read him thoroughly, or to give a fair guess at the employment of his cogitations."

If this had been the extent of her revelations, then had she been pardonable; but those whose tongues run so mercilessly, will, behind their backs, find something still to say, more than the truth, to the injury of their neighbors. This is to be a backbiter, and a backbiter is a detractor, and a detractor is a slanderer, and a *slanderer* is the devil.

When they returned to the castle, they met young Van Corts, with the Burgher, at the gate. He was introduced to Belinda, but declined a pressing invitation to walk in; promising, however, to do so at some future time. The dark eye of Belinda had pierced him; the sudden twitch she gave his hand had extended to the fibres of his heart, and he was already within love's inextricable meshes.

> Belinda "sure was formed without a spot,
> Nature in her then erred not — but forgot,
> With every pleasing, every prudent part.
> What can" Belinda "want? — She wants a heart." — *Pope*.

Sunday morning had arrived, the sun was walking majestically up the sky, the zephyrs were whispering among the trees, while the singing of birds and the chiming of church bells soothed the mind and predisposed it for the duties of the day.

It was not till the house was nearly filled that Belinda and her aunt came into the chapel. All eyes were turned towards the *fair stranger* as she with perfect grace walked up the aisle. Whether to attract attention or by accident, she appeared to have some difficulty in opening the door of her pew. The button was turned too far and then too far back again and again, not *intentionally* of course. She knew Fitz Rowland from the description she had had of his person, the cut of his coat, and the shape of his whiskers, and, as she took her seat, her speaking eyes dwelt a moment — only a moment — upon him; but a thrust of the assassin's dagger, would not have been more instantaneously effective. The wound was one which "no drug, no time, no argument could cure!"*****Her appearance was sanctimonious, and her voice in singing melodious and clear.

The closest attention was paid to the preacher and the text, with the principal divisions of the sermon, was entered in her memorandum book.

When the service was ended young Rowland requested the Burgher to give him an "introduction to the strange lady who had looked so invitingly and sung so sweetly." He was accordingly made acquainted with Belinda at the door, where Van Corts also shook her by the hand; but neither of them presumed any farther at that time.

Rowland's thoughts were continually upon the beauty — the passing beauty — of the dark eyed stranger. He no sooner went home than he confessed his admiration of her to his mother and sisters, but it was not natural to suppose that they should be equally taken with her. His heart, however, was fixed, true as the needle to the pole, without being subject even to its variations. A few evenings after this as Belinda was walking musingly and languidly along the bank of the river she was overtaken by Rowland who offered her his arm, which she at first seemed to decline, and the next moment declared herself very happy in accepting. Rowland remarked that it was a delightful evening. Belinda answered that she always felt a propensity to adore when she walked forth in the evening; — "to see the stars winking like eyes of intelligence — the azure sky in the west where Phoebus has not yet withdrawn his rays; and pale Cynthia gently climbing up the steep of heaven, always effect me with sensations of gratitude, as well as of wonder. I cannot contemplate them without praising their maker, and the bounteous giver of every benefit we enjoy."

"Your language is the language of poetry," replies Rowland. "It affects me with the power of magic. I partake of your spirit while I hang upon your tongue. The sky, the stars and the moon, with the author of them all, appear more beautiful, more worthy of admiration and of adoration, from the hearing of your description. And now, my dear, had I *your* graphic powers at command, I'd tell you how I love you! not how much — that is impossible — but how sincerely. Yes, Belinda, I love thee, and although my tongue was never formed for adulation, nor my lips for flattery, yet your exquisite beauty, but more particularly the excellent qualities of your mind, and the amiable dispositions, — which I read in your phisiognomy — have quite conquered my natural caution and indecision. The first time I saw your face was the first time that I ever admired one in my life!"

"Now," exclaims Miss Howard, "I do firmly believe
'There's a divinity that slopes our ends,
 Rough hew them as we will,'
for what but a superintending and all-wise Providence could have conducted me to this place to be so highly honored? I only wish that I were worthy to become the partner of your joys and sorrows, but I do not aspire after such an elevation — it is beyond my utmost ambition."

"You stand already upon an eminence above the rest of your sex, and, consequently, have not much prospect of advancing to a more honorable station by any connection you may form; but, my love, if you will accept my hand, I shall consider myself the happiest, and most fortunate of men."

"It appears to me like a dream, so much beyond the most extravagant of all my hopes. I do thank you very kindly, sir, for the notice you have taken of me — a stranger. I never before knew what it was to be from home; it is a melancholy, almost a painful, feeling, but the unpleasantness of my situation will be much mollified, and indeed, become paradisiacal, if in you I find a friend to whom I can confide my most secret thoughts." By this time they had returned to the gate. Rowland raised her hand to his lips, and bid her a very good night, promising to visit the castle in a week from that evening. She courtesied, but said nothing, and they parted. Belinda was met at the door by her aunt, who inquired what had kept her out so late in the cold night air. She answered that she had been met by Rowland, heard from him an avowal of love, and might, had she been so disposed, have sealed a contract of marriage that very night. "He is very clever; I shall be glad to retain him for a time, at least, as a beau. I will receive his company again at a stated time." Her aunt clasped her hands in an ecstacy of joy, that the tiresome monotony of her house was about changing, and in a way most congenial to her disposition, informed Belinda that Van Corts had been invited by her to spend the next evening with them, and hoped she would be able to while away the tedious hours without actually committing herself. The monstrous earth soon wheeled once around upon its axis, making sleeping men the antipodes of their waking selves, and Van Corts arrived and was made very welcome by the ladies at the castle.

The subject of conversation was changed rapidly as ladies knew how — the state of the weather, the price of silks and satins, their friends, their enemies, the young, the old, love, murder, wedding parties and funeral processions, all helped to fill a niche in time, till the clock struck eleven, and not a word could be remembered. The Burgher and his lady had now retired. Van Corts began to feel as if everything had been said, but Miss Howard fortunately could talk without thinking at all. With her usual ambiguity she paid him many compliments, which he of course was bound to return without measure. He at last rose to take his leave, but not without having agreed upon a second conference to be held, with closed doors, in which very important matters were to be considered, it being understood at the same time that there would remain but very little to be *settled* upon the occasion. The time was not appointed. This was an oversight of Belinda, who, like the all-grasping Corsican, generally formed her plans with consummate judgment and the most profound sagacity, but now and then made an egregious blunder.

The appointed time for the visit of Rowland had arrived, and Belinda was standing in thoughtful mood in the porch of the castle. Every thing at that moment was arrayed in a sable mantle — buildings, woods and hills had faded from the view, while it appeared as if the messengers of propitious heaven were employed in lighting up ten thousand brilliant lamps to adorn the concave sky, and to point man from nature still onward and upward. Not a breeze was stirring, not a sound was heard, except the lonely tones of whip-poor-will, and the distant croakings of loquacious frogs. Belinda, seeing a gentleman ride up, and supposing it to be Rowland, prudently retired to her room; but she was not prepared for the dilemma in which she was placed when he was ushered in. It was Van Corts, who then expected the fulfilment of what she had promised him should take place at some indefinite time. The door again opened and Fitz Rowland, who was naturally suspicious, entered the room and took his seat between Miss Howard and the contumacious Dutchman.

The Burgher's lady was a proficient in what

Shakspeare calls the "hold door trade," but she had out-generaled herself when she had brought together a company consisting of parts so entirely incongruous. 'Twas worse a thousand times for each one present, than if he or she had been alone. All were silent as the grave, or if one spoke, the words dragged slowly and heavily as an anchor clutched in old ocean's bottom. Van Corts and Rowland looked bitter things each at the other, and harbored dark designs within the deep recesses of their bosoms. Belinda, not yet satisfied to give up one forever, by showing a decided partiality for the other, put on a matronal and saintly air, and began to talk about the pleasure and indispensible necessity of religion. Her observations were correct and beautiful, and as she showed no particular respect for either of her votaries; her scheme was completely successful. And although her "face was too grave, her prayers too long," yet they both believed her to be nothing less than an embodied angel. About nine o'clock, Van Corts, saying that he had no intention of stopping so late when he came in, hastily took his leave. All reserve was immediately banished. Rowland declared that she had not been out of his thoughts, sleeping or waking, five minutes since he first saw her, and again importunately pushes the question of his fate, or whether she would consent to become that night his affianced wife. Belinda answered, that even that modesty which was suitable for her sex could no longer maintain that complete ascendency which had till now prevented her from confessing the violence of the flame that was kindled in her heart. "There are only two things," said she, "which I wish to ascertain before I can, and satisfy my own conscience, enter into a solemn vow. One is whether you, my dear Rowland, are a firm believer in the great truths of revelation; whether you will, for my sake, join yourself in close communion with the church, and consent to live a Godly, righteous and sober life. For we are commanded 'not to be unequally yoked with the unbelieving;' besides; is not the thought a most terrifying one, of being united in this world, and separated in the next? The other is the will of my dear parents, but I expect to return home in a few weeks, and am confident there will be no objection when they are consulted."

"Nothing could yield me more complete satisfaction," said Rowland, "than to perceive your solicitude for my future happiness. This makes me believe that you love me, and if you *wish* me happy, why not *make* me so while you have it your power?"

"If your fate were in my hands, felicity should mark each moment of your life."

"It is in your hands for this world, to say the least, Belinda!"

"Then you are blessed."

While thus engaged they counted no time, and, ere they suspected an hour spent, shrill chanticleer proclaimed the dawn, and looking from the window they perceived aurora already streaking the east. Rowland rose to take his leave. Belinda urged him to remain but half an hour longer, while vows of love and ever during constancy were many times repeated. He said "I hope your mind will never change — I hope you will be always true." "You hope I will be true!" exclaims Miss Howard, starting upon her feet, "why then, you deem it possible I should be false? If every feeling of your heart were absorbed, like mine, in love, you would have confidence." "Time will prove the stability of my love. You are all I wish you to be, only remain such. Farewell."

> "Did he once look or lend a listening ear,
> Sighed when I sobbed, or shed one kindly tear,
> All symptoms of a base ungrateful mind;
> So bad that which is worse 'tis hard to find.
> I rave! I rave!" — *Dryden's Virgil.*

The last words of Fitz Rowland sank deep into Belinda's heart. That he loved her she did not doubt; but the words *"be true,"* still sounded in her ears. She feared that something which he had seen or heard might have induced him thus gently to chide her. He had found her that evening in the company of Van Corts, and the story of her intercourse with Mack and others at the Clifton Hall might have reached his ears. She now recollected his size, shape, features, complexion, all precisely such as she would have chosen in a companion for life. She felt as if she were about to be deserted. Custom may forbid the sex the privilege of making the first advances in certain cases, but no demon of the air may prevent their speaking afterwards. This was instanced in the conduct of the fond Belinda. Rowland had requested her to walk hand in hand with him through life. She had provisionally consented; and nothing should now hinder her from throwing herself at his feet, at the first opportunity, and praying him to save her from dying of a broken heart, or from becoming an inmate of the lunatic asylum. Her industrious and excited mind soon completed an extensive and intricate plan of operations. She had been invited by the sisters of Fitz Rowland to take tea with them the next Tuesday afternoon, and after tea she might *take sick*, if in her discretion it would be calculated to advance the business of the day.

The tea party she accordingly attended, and Rowland, who was very differently disposed towards her from what she had imagined, placed himself so as to have a fair view of her as she came in, without being observed himself. He could compare her to nothing but the celebrated Egyptian queen, when she went to visit Mark Anthony.(Well had it been for thee, Belinda, had the likeness extended no farther than to the features of thy face.) Her silken hair fell in ringlets on her shoulders, a continual smile dwelt upon her countenance; every gesture, every motion was dignity and love — heaven beamed in her eye, the colors of the rose and lilly were displayed in her cheeks and forehead. This, however, was the judgment of a lover, and love is blind and deaf, and consequently liable to err.

It was not till tea was on the table that Rowland made his appearance, and even then he did not appear to be prepossessed in favor of any particular one of the company, or to treat Belinda with greater deference than any other individual present, all which struck her as the fulfilling of her forebodings. She was thoughtful and demure, and, just as the company was about to disperse, complained of a severe pain in the head — became nervous and agitated. Her eyes, which were before so steady, became unfixed and rolled about from object to object, and she at last fainted away in the arms of Rowland, who conveyed her into another apartment, and laid her upon a bed. She soon revived so as to be able to speak; expressed great uneasiness at being unable to go home, and was afraid that her remaining would give rise to unpleasant remarks from those who were unacquainted with the circumstances of the case. While Roland was by her bed-side she was cheerful and talkative, but no sooner was he out of her sight than she would swoon, fall into a lethargy, or become delirious, and call for her father, her mother, or for Rowland. This continued several days, during which time she would frequently inquire of those about her what Rowland's intentions were, whether he still loved her, or whether he intended to deceive her. He solemnly protested that her fears were without foundation, that every thing depended upon herself, and that she might as reasonably expect the eternal hills to change their posture and positions as that his mind should waver, or his heart lose its tendency to love her. Her eyes would follow him as he moved across the room, and as soon as he was absent, she would sink back and exclaim "he is gone!" She would then arraign her hard fate, ask if Rowland was not coming back, what his feelings towards her were, and how he spoke of her when he was out of her hearing. The continual assurances which she received of his affectionate regards, and of his intention to make her his wife, at length in some degree pacified her; and as her peace of mind returned, the debility of her body ceased, so that by Saturday morning she was able to set up, or walk about the room. At this critical period, Mrs. Howard, Belinda's grandmother, who had been traveling in the south for her health, and to see, for the last time, those of her children who were residing in the United States, (where she also spent her pristine days before that great nation had a name,) visited the castle of the old Burgher. By his lady she was soon made acquainted with the circumstance of her favorite, Belinda, having been taken suddenly and dangerously ill at the house of Fitz Rowland, about half a league from the castle, but that she was now convalescent, and that if a carriage were sent down that day, it was to be hoped her niece would be able to return home. "Fitz Rowland," she added, "is entirely destitute of all those qualifications which I admire in a man, and yet he has entirely seduced her affections, and gained a complete ascendency over her mind. He neither makes a showy, or noble appearance, nor is refined in his addresses — is neither generous nor gallant, and yet the dear, mistaken Belinda loves him tenderly, passionately, madly. But what vexes me more than all the rest," she cried, "is the disrespectful manner in which myself have been treated by Fitz Rowland, together with the thoughts that I first recommended him to her favorable notice. I did it innocently, because I did it ignorantly — judging of him from the fame of his father, I presumed he would prove an example of the picture I had in my eye of a complete gentleman. But he has deceived me. I am becoming acquainted with the people of this neighborhood; the men are a base, degenerate race, and the women are the most hideous frights the world ever saw." The old lady, who had become quite tired of listening to a tale from one in whom she had no confidence; and who, she knew, was very fond of using that figure of speech which Rhetoricians call hyperbole, said she had a distinct recollection of the Rev. Fitz Rowland — was herself under infinitie obligations to him, and that his like, take him all in all, she never hoped to see again. She knew it was foolish to respect the son for the virtues of his father, but how nonsensical soever it might sound, yet she could not help saying that the name was to her an honored name, and that if young Rowland was in any way worthy of it, then it followed that he was also worthy of Belinda. Notwithstanding her favorable impressions of the Rowland family, she was very desirious of seeing Belinda, and proposed that her own coach should be immediately sent — it would be necessary, however, as she must be still quite weak, that some person besides a servant, some confidential person, with whom she was familiar, be requested to go. She might not be able to set up in the coach without assistance.

The Burgher's lady manifested some degree of surprise that her word should not be taken — hoped that her veracity was not doubted, and begged implicit confidence while she gave the character of Van Corts, for whom she had already sent. "I speak from personal knowledge, and do most positively affirm that besides him there is not a decent young man within a circle of ten miles. Van Corts is obliging in his disposition and condescending in his demeanor, agreeable in company, and full of good humor, cheerful, lively, animated! His father, (everybody's uncle,) is an old *residenter* in the place, as rich as a Jew, very respectable, and, above suspicion, a truly good man. This young gentleman, too, loves Belinda; he has made some advances, and she has given him no small encouragement; he therefore has a right to push his claims, and I am prepared to favor his pretensions. My words shall be to his like a body of reserve in an army; while Rowland, if he advance, shall feel the heaviest lashes of my tongue." The ancient matron, although her blood had almost stopped its circulation and three score wrinkles streaked her face — yet hanged her head and, for the honor of her sex, blushed to the eyes once more before she died.

Van Corts was come. He felt some delicacy in going on such an errand, and particularly to the house of Fitz Rowland, but the woman with a tongue soon persuaded him to undertake the expedition. He leaped into the coach, and like Jehu, dashed forward, neck or nought. When he drove into the yard, Rowland came out and informed him that Belinda was yet very far from well, but invited him to walk in. He instantly complied. In a large room, across a spacious bed, in full dress, the pale Belinda lay, and as Van Corts entered he thought she looked like breathless Dido on her funeral pile with her sister beside her. When she knew that her grandmother was at her uncle's and had sent for her, she declared her determination, although more than usually faint just then, to go and see her without delay. With the assistance of Rowland's mother, she succeeded in rising, and being seated in a chair, Van Corts took her by the hand and said he was very sorry to see her so unwell, but, as the morning was extremely fine, he hoped a short ride in the open air would do her good. A sight of the broad and smiling face of nature would raise her depressed spirits; and the fanning of the western breezes, with a little exercise, would soon restore the lost carnation of her cheek. He drew endless arguments from the anxiety of her infirm grandmother — her having visited all her children, and her wishes to see Belinda before returning home, and from the almost peremptory commands of her aunt. All this was true, but Rowland imagined that he could see through the specious veil into the regions beyond. The persuasive reasonings of Van Corts, it could not be denied, were succinct and clear, but his competitor for the prize knew well that "there are more things in heaven and earth than are dreamed of in philosophy." The one appeared quite disinterested and unconcerned, and said he cared not for his own individual self, whether he were accompanied by

Miss Howard in his return or not; the other was observant, vigilant, suspicious.

Fitz Rowland determined upon giving Belinda to understand his wishes, that she should at present remain, and from her consequent actions, as a criterion, to judge of the genuineness of her love. Her quick eye perceived his meaning ere he spoke. She fainted in her chair, creating a great alarm; was laid again upon the bed, and as soon as it was perceptible that breath and pulse remained, and that the precious life of the lovely Belinda was not quite extinct, Van Corts respectfully, but silently, took his leave. About half an hour had elapsed, when she again revived and sat up, talked of her grandmother, her unfortunate situation that she should be thus debarred, by her inability to ride, from seeing her; said she felt better than she had any time during the week — got up and walked to the window, thought she might now go home if she had an opportunity, or if the coach of her grandmother had not left so quickly. Fitz Rowland ordered his own carriage with a cheerful countenance, and with a quick and springy step she left the house and was handed in, and by the time they drove up at the castle gate every symptom of her disease had disappeared.

Fitz Rowland now, in his own heart's estimation, was completely prosperous and completely happy, and yet, like the ghost of Aeneis' father, his fate would often stare him in the face, and in his most pleasurable moments, make him tremble for the dark impenetrable future. As they parted he again repeated those ominous and frightful words, "be constant, be true." Belinda avered that love so pure, so deep, so continuous, so disinterested and heartfelt, so unconstrained and violent, and yet so platonic, was never, never, since our fair world left its chaotic state, known once to change, or cease to be, but with the life of her who loves; nay, not even then. "I have not," said she, "the shadow of a doubt that we shall love when we meet in those elevated climes where the expanded views will at once our narrow minds expand. And while we praise Him who without any adequate return from us, first loved us — bought us with a great price, and graciously brought us thither — I believe that we will feel ties in some respects similar to those which now so indissolubly make us one." She then gave him her hand, and said she should never forget, and felt satisfied he would not, that "This is the hand which, by a vowed contract, 'was fast belocked in thine.'" Rowland gave it what he fancied would prove three secure seals to the bargain; and as the voice of Belinda's *duenna* was heard, he said "you will, I know you will remain, my love, loyal, constant, true — good bye." She entered the castle and Fitz Rowland was on his way home.

The same afternoon of Belinda's return to the seat of the old Burgher, as she sat at her chamber window, she saw drive into the yard what she in a moment identified as her father's carriage from the Clifton Hall. In it were two gentlemen of familiar appearance — they proved to be her elder brother Brock, and her old lover, McLeod, the Scotchman. The reader must carefully distinguish betweeen this McLeod, and him who afterwards carried on a more successful courtship at Navy Island, out-Yankeyed Brother Jonathan himself, placed the two greatest Christian nations on the earth in a rampant posture, and so narrowly escaped being rewarded for his temerity with a halter at New York. Belinda had the greatest satisfaction, she said, in seeing her brother and making him welcome at the castle, but he must pardon her if her pleasure was still greater at the unexpected visit of her dear Mack. She asked a thousand questions about her parents, sisters, cousins, neighbors, without giving time to answer one, and at last inquired of Mack in a whisper, whether that impertinent jackanapes, Barnabas, had ever, since she left, shown his booby's face.

"Why Mack, you have changed wonderfully since I saw you; you have grown an inch or two, upon my word. If you could be guilty of a wrong, I'd say you have sinned in keeping away so long — it seems to me like five years, and yet it is scarce so many months."

Mack was highly flattered by the agreeable temper in which he happened to find the mutable Belinda. He thought the world was all his own, and that his possession of what he had so long labored to obtain was now certain. She had been so long absent, seen so many strangers, who must have admired her incomparable beauty of form and feature; and yet, to all appearance, loved him as sincerely as ever she had done. Mack asked her how she liked the people of the neighborhood. With a deep sigh, she replied that the opinion she had formed from casual passers-by, and from the little chance she had had of becoming acquainted with a few young ladies, was not particularly favorable. She admitted, however, that her opportunities of knowing were not sufficient to enable her to judge with any degree of certainty. As to the young gentlemen, she was apt to think them very much uncultivated, from the fact that not one of them had more than passed the time of day with her since her residence in the castle. The family having dined previous to their arrival, the table was quickly prepared for Howard and Mack, who, setting down, Belinda walked out. By a singular coincidence, Mr. John Baptist Swift, a cashier, with whom she had become acquainted when at home at her father's, and for whom she had also formed a *very particular attachment*, rode up to the gate on horseback, just as Miss Howard went out and not an hour after Mack, from the same place, on the same business, and with the same well grounded hopes, had arrived at the castle.

The communication between Belinda and the cashier commenced some time during the preceding winter, soon after the discomfiture of Barnabas. It had been carried on principally by letters, and he had consequently escaped becoming obnoxious to the suspicion of Mack. But there must now be some manouvreing, or an engagement would be inevitable. Swift had no sooner dismounted, then she stepped from the door to greet him, expressing her joy at so unhoped-for a meeting. "My dearest Belinda," said the cashier, as he took his seat beside her on a sofa in the hall, "I love you as I long have, and as I am sure I can never love another; indeed, it seems to me impossible that I should cease to love you, and not cease to be the same man. The heart, that feels no attraction towards you must be different from the one which my Maker has planted within my frame; the eye, which is not charmed with a single view of your exquisitely chiseled features, cannot be of the same organization with mine; and the mind which has nothing congenial to yours, by no metamorphosis whatever, can be the one that I possess. My regard for you then, Belinda, to say the least, is necessary to my identity, if not essential to my being. May I not say that you have often, in your invaluable epistles, told me, by direct inference, that you loved me, and only me? And now, if I should hear those words flow from your angel tongue, and be assured that they came from the seat of life and thought, then should I be fully remunerated for a long, rough route, and many guineas spent."

Belinda, with a seeming blush, replied "my heart and self, and all I have are yours, I love you, only you, and never did I or can another love. My heart was fixed one year ago this day by the receipt of your first letter. I touched my lips to your name, and vowed the hand that wrote it should, when it closed, grasp mine. Since that day, the happiest of my life, I've loved you, dearest sir, without one moment's insipidity or cessation. But I forgot to tell you that my brother has come hither and brought with him (as teamster I suppose or lackey) that gabbleing blockhead, Mack. In his appearance he is the greatest scarecrow I ever saw, I wish my uncle would send him to the fields to frighten the birds away. He is a

Scotchman — there are many clever men among the Scotch, but this base, lowborn pretender, I'm satisfied, has caught, and lived on herring all his life."

The Burgher coming out at this moment, Belinda, after making him acquainted with the Cashier, retired to her own apartments, and was not seen again by the party that evening. The Cashier congratulated himself with the idea that she had such a detestation of the very sight of Mack that she would not sit in the same room where he was — even though her brother and himself, her lover, were present. Mack supposed the reason for her absence to be because she had seen the Cashier when he came in to the castle and, anticipating the object of his visit, had determined to show him no countenance. By this device she consequently raised herself still higher in their estimation, while she treated them both with the most contemptuous neglect.

The next morning being Sunday, Belinda appeared at the breakfast table as serious and thoughtful as if she had been standing at her mother's grave — she said that she had been reading several Psalms and had caught the spirit of the Psalmist; "how thankful we should be for sanctuary privileges and how religiously we should devote the fore part of the day, not only to dressing our bodies but to the putting of our minds in a suitable frame for receiving instruction."

This secured her from receiving any proposals for private conversation that morning, and of course from being obliged to show a preference for either of the gentlemen present.

The Chapel being but a few steps from the Burgher's door, the whole family started on foot; and Belinda, by waiting upon her grandmother, not only performed a filial duty but prevented either Mack or the Cashier from tendering the same assistance to herself.

At church Belinda had the indescribable pleasure

of seeing all her beaux together. They formed a splendid corps — comely, noble, valiant, and worthy to stand before a queen. Towards Fitz Rowland she turned a look of languishment, gave half a smile to young Van Corts, and the other half to Kellogue; made a dimple in her chin for Mac, and gently raised her brows to the Cashier. Each one said to himself "I am a monarch of all I survey, my right there is none to dispute," and perhaps scarcely thought the house dedicated to a greater than *himself*. Were they idolators? They were not Polytheists; their thoughts dwelt upon, and they worshiped one only god; — but who was that god and where was his heaven? Ay, there's the rub! This might now, if one had a little leisure, be worth an hour's sober thinking. The sermon was soon ended, and those who kept a book and pencil might tell, when they went home, where the text was to be found. Fitz Rowland, at the door, shook hands with Belinda and walked near her to the castle gate, though a little out of his way. He was glad to see her health so rapidly improving, but "hoped she would not make our pleasant vale a desert by returning with her brother." At this the Scotchman pricked his ears, and, so amazed was he that his eyes looked like the boding night bird's, when, in the thicket, he is disturbed by day. The afternoon was passed much as the morning had been; the company at the castle resembled some assemblages of politicians which I remember having seen in revolutionary times, where tory, whig, and rebel indiscriminately mingled, and each one kept an eye upon his neighbor's sleeve for fear of secret dirks or pistols. The evening found them again at the place where truth is dispensed and Fitz Rowland, as he had been before, was unaccountably bold; he even walked nearer than in the morning, and, although it was very dark, Mack said he half believed Belinda took his arm. Rowland asked her if she knew who those two strange gentlemen were, or what part of the country they were from?

She answered that she had heard one of their names mentioned by her brother but not having paid any attention to it had quite forgotten it; the other she believed to be a cashier of some bank down the country. "I have not," she continued, "inquired what his business is with my uncle, nor do I know any thing of his character; but my first impressions were very unfavorable; I hope my uncle will have no dealings with him; I would not be afraid to pledge my jewels that he is an exceeding knave, although I never saw him before nor have spoken to him yet. He is a smutty, sottish, soulless, sordid, sour, sly, slovenly, sneaking, sort of a speculator."

"Let us," said Rowland, impatiently, as if afraid to allow her to proceed for fear of being convinced of her duplicity, "exchange vows once more before we part, I love thee still and purpose honorable marriage as soon as may be to us both convenient."

"I love you, Rowland, more than I can tell, and am prepared, at your own time, to have a priest join our hands as God has already united our hearts. Yes, only say the word, my dearest Rowland, and I will leave every other friend I have on earth and follow you around the world."

The Cashier inquired who that was that accompanied them to the gate? Belinda answered, "I was just about to ask the same question of my uncle. I cannot conceive who he can be. His voice is entirely strange to me; his conduct too is very mysterious. If we had had a dozen steps farther to go I would have told the intrusive blockhead that his company was not agreeable. I wonder if he could have been the same pretty man who insulted me this morning by pretending an acquaintance; and intimated that I had been sick, and looked bad still, by saying he was glad to see my health so much improved." Belinda wished them all good night and instantly retired. Mack slept not one half hour that whole night, and the next morning, knowing Miss Howard to be an early riser, he came down stairs before the shades of night had altogether disappeared. Belinda met him in the hall and, with pleasant countenances, a thousand compliments were passed. She hoped he would spend the week with them it was so solitary at the castle, when she was all alone. They would enjoy a country ride so well together, or a short walk just as day's King sets all the eastern horizon on fire would be so very pleasant.

"I am compelled by business, to return immediately. Your brother and myself must leave as soon as we have breakfasted. But this pains me not, since we leave not you, but take you with us. And on those lofty shore, where our hearts, by pure affection, were first amalgamated, while ever murmuring waters wash the stones beneath our feet, we'll many pleasant summer evenings spend."

"My dear, dear, Mack, your rich fancy makes me love you more and more each time I hear you speak. You have put my spirits in a glow. I'm sure if you should give imagination its full scope, my poet, you would better write than Scott, or Burns. I am resolved, if my aunt consent, to go with you this day."

Just at this moment Brock came down, and calling to Mack, informed him that he had some business to transact with Van Corts, and would be glad of his assistance. The house was only half a mile away, and they might very soon return. Mack consented, bidding Belinda "good bye, but not forever."

"Brock," said he, "your sister has agreed to leave the stiff and stingy Burgher, and his borough, and go home with us, providing only that her aunt consent, which I am sure she will."

To this, Brock replied in words full of meaning. "That, now, sir, is precisely like some *other things* of which you are *sure!* I tell you she will not consent, and Belinda, consequently, will remain, and we return alone."

Brock had become acquainted with Rowland, and, by means of his grandmother, with all that had passed between him and Belinda, and was already prepossessed in his favor, and in favor of a connection being formed with the family.

It was late before the cashier came down stairs; but he knew how many shillings it takes to make a pound, as well as Mack did the number of square inches in the superfices of a lady's foot.

After giving and receiving the usual compliments, he handed Belinda the following, which he had written that morning. It was dated,

> The Castle in the Valley,
> Monday Morning.

"My Dear Belinda — When we are irresistably compelled to act, we cannot, for that action, be culpable. I presume, therefore, that you will consider my addressing you as a thing quite pardonable, when you know that my hand very reluctantly performs its office — that my reason almost refuses to supply me with language; but that the violence of my love engages all the members of my body and faculties of my soul in its service, and with a power which nothing can oppose, urges me forward either to my own destruction or felicity. Which shall it be, Belinda? My fate is in your hands. My object here is to settle the preliminaries of our marriage, and to know when the consummation shall take place. To-day, my business calls me hence, and I have not yet had an opportunity of speaking with you on the subject. I love you — you have told me that my love is returned. What, then, remains to prevent us from becoming one in name, as we are in heart?

"Please drop me a line, immediately on receiving this, and let me know your never-changing mind.

"Your truest lover,

"J.B. Swift."

To this, Belinda, without five minutes thought, returned the subjoined singular, and difficult-to-be-understood answer:

Monday Morning, 9 o'clock.

"Dear Sir — I do not know whether to call what has just been handed me, a piece of good advice, a petition for favors merited, or a command artfully couched. Your paper, however, has been read the third time and laid upon the table; your words have received due consideration; the substance of them is digested, and lies hid in the deepest recess of my fluttering heart. You have love enough, but rather too much logic. Some of your expressions are very plain and unequivocal. This, a distinguishing trait in your character, I admire above every other quality in a man. For, (maugre what is taunting in your lines,) I think of you, more than my pen will at present consent to write. I am sorry if you must leave this part of the country so soon. I thought we should have spent many happy hours together ere you left.

"You wish to know my *never changing mind.* To this, my dear Baptist, I can only say that mine is most emphatically a *never changing mind.* I shall return to the Clifton Hall in two or three weeks, where I sincerely hope to see you often.

"Till which time, in amity and love,
          Believe me, truly yours,
                    "BELINDA."

"Mr. J.B. Swift."

When the cashier read Miss Howard's letter, he felt like a criminal, who, having been condemned to death, has a reprieve of three days granted him, with a faint hope that even then, the sentence will not be carried into execution. Indeed, it appeared that Miss H. had rather lost than gained with the cashier — though as he gave her the parting salute, he whispered, (for Mack was by,) "I love thee still;" she answered in a voice still lower, "ditto, and I thank you, sir." These few words again blew the flame into a ten fold rage. Mack was assured that woman's love was an unalterable thing, and that he soon would prove it. The company took their leave.

It was about a fortnight after the visit of McLeod and Swift at the castle, that Fitz Rowland called to see the only one whom he thought worthy to be loved among the many millions of her sex. He, apologizing for his long absence, said the business of a very urgent nature had obliged him, the next morning after he had seen her last, to proceed directly to the seat of government; and that on his return he spent a day and night at the Clifton hall. He had been made acquainted with *"our father and mother;"* had intimated to them his expectation and intention of becoming a member of their family; and received the most encouraging marks of respect and esteem from them both, and also from Brock. One of those gentlemen whom he saw at the castle, two weeks ago, was at her father's. They called him Mack. He believed, from what he had learned from her brother, that Mack was permanently residing at the Clifton Hall. Her father was desirous that she should return home before a great while, and perhaps might come himself after her in a few days. "But if he do, Belinda, just touch my heart once more with the loadstone of your love, and I will find you out, though you travel to more northern realms than ever have been in this hemisphere explored."

"You cannot doubt my love, nor do I yours. If you should prove false, a thing even in supposition impossible, I never would believe another word that any man might say, how fair soever he appeared. I would shut my eyes, and stop my ears, and to my grave I would blindly and deafly rush, in a state of single blessedness, in spite of all that all the men on earth could do. I love you, and I will become your wife, your *everlasting wife*, I care not how soon."

"I love you, above comparison, Belinda, and will become your husband, if you never change your mind. So help me God!"

About a week after this last repetition of frightful vows, Esquire Howard arrived at the castle of the old Burgher, and his fair daughter accompanied him home. It ought to be remarked, however, that, before leaving, he sent his ticket, with his compliments, to Fitz Rowland. Nothing could surpass the beauty of the prospect that now presented itself to their view; for the works of nature very far exceed those of art, not only in the largeness of the whole, but in the variety of the parts, and both nature and art appeared to have done their best for the romantic valley through which Belinda and her father were now traveling. A noble river, on which steamers were continually plying, calculated to strike beholders with their exterior beauty and rapid motion, seemed just then to lie motionless, like a serpent basking in the summer sun. Here and there stood a stately brig or schooner, with all its wingy sails extended, waiting the soft breezes to waft it to its destination. Equa-distant on each bank, were neat and comfortable mansions; and the spaces between them filled with orchards of all kinds of fruit trees in full bloom, and flapping their foliage with pure delight. The whole country round, as far as the eye could reach, covered with fields of richest hues, without one isolated spot of stony ground to spoil the scene. Every garden, and every grove, betokened plenty, and whispered peace.

CHAPTER IV.

When the carriage of Esq. Howard drove up at the Clifton Hall, Mack was at the wheel to hand Belinda down, but the activity of her brother, superceded any such necessity. Brock's conduct on the occasion was not altogether respectful, and it tended very materially to widen the breach which was already made between him and the sensitive Mack. But it was the ruin of Belinda, as it has been of thousands besides, and will be of all who practice it, that she would admit, and thought it rightful prerogative to admit, to her private company, all who had the assurance to make the request. The language of love was at all times, and from every empty noddle, made welcome, and even encouraged, from the merry-andrew himself. Her ear, by this means, became too familiar, for a virtuous woman, with the obscene language of persons of vicious habits; her delicate sense, by which she could once distinguish between proper and improper conduct, became vitiated; and her fall from the envied superiority which she enjoyed was fast approaching!

But her time had not yet come; she was to bask a little while longer in the sunshine of favor, and then retire to the shades of infamy forever; she still could pass, with her pretty face and silver voice, among those of good repute, and characters unsmirched, but his satanic majesty himself cannot supply that cunning which must be brought into requisition, to make vice always prosperous. This, it will become my duty to exemplify, in the case of the unfortunate Belinda.

Mack had taken rooms near the Clifton Hall and paid his board with Esq. Howard.

The Cashier had a fine estate about five leagues off, from which his carriage was known to drive to the Clifton Hall with a *speaking* frequency and regularity.

Mr. S. lived with his father fifty miles in an opposite direction from the Hall; and Mr. K. the cosmopolite appeared in the immediate neighborhood very frequently. Belinda had an uncle in the vicinity, — her father's brother, — at whose house she used to pass much of her time, and receive, pursuant to appointment, the company of those whom she supposed her parents would not approve. Here she often met S., giving, as was her custom, every encouragement, but at last refusing his offers, and rejecting him with disdain.

One week after Belinda's return home from the Burgher's, she was very agreeably surprised by seeing Fitz Rowland ride into the yard. She ran out to meet him with the most extravagant demonstrations of joy. "I was apprehensive," said she, "when I left the valley that we should never see each other again; but now my fears of any reverse of fortune are utterly banished and my happiness is as nearly perfect as it can possibly be upon this our globe." What one unthinkingly affirmed, the other actually felt. They walked into the house hand in hand. Rowland was received by the rest of the family like a son and brother. There was only one thing that afternoon which in any measure annoyed or chafed him, and that was the presence, at the tea table, of the Scotchman, McLeod, who was officious in helping Belinda to every dish that he could reach; and who spoke several times to her in an undertone of voice!

After tea Belinda and Rowland retired to a private room where she unhesitatingly showed him the following letter which had just been received from

the post when he came in. It was dated,
> Wesleyan Cottage, May 9th, 1833.

To My Sweetheart — As I love you and believe that you have the same feelings towards me, though perhaps not in the same degree, I presume no apology will be necessary for my sending you a few lines.

Every thing appears to wear a different aspect since you left us. The blossoms are beginning to fade and fall from the trees; heavy clouds roll across the sky, hiding the sun by day and the moon and stars by night; and we all stalk dull and gloomy along the streets, as if we had been notified from heaven that some dreadful calamity was impending. I sat down this afternoon to scrutinize and examine into the cause of my own melancholy, and can attribute it to nothing but your absence and can discover no other cure but the restoration of your presence. I consequently determined to write and to let you know there is, among the ten thousand who admire your beauty, one who loves you from his heart and who would make any sacrifice to obtain your hand.

There is one thing which I cannot forbear mentioning before I close my letter though I feel it to be a very delicate subject. *Every thing that every man says ought not to be believed. If we always rely with implicit confidence upon his professions we shall often be imposed upon.* Please write me soon — at least send these three words *"I love you."*
> Your lover,   Van Corts.

"Now," says Belinda, "these three words for which Van Corts begs would make quite a laconic letter. But they are very significant words; many a volume has been published without so much information between its lids as might be conveyed by these three monosylables. I had rather write a book myself and fill it full of long, hard, ambiguous and unpronouncable words, than once to use those same three. I will not, cannot write them, I never wrote them in my life — nor spoke them to any man between the poles, with one only, solitary, exception; and that exception was yourself, my dearest Rowland. I can say them now — *I love you.*"

"If you love *me*, and I doubt not you do, commit that letter to the flames. It will be like separating the pure metal from the dross. It will be pruning yourself from an excrescence which lessens your attractions. I would not give a groat for a fraction of love though it were ever so near unity. Like the ambitious Macedonian I must have all or none. The planetary system has only one sun, and a woman must have but one lover. Love is indivisible!"

"Is it not possible then for me to love you, and at the same time to love my parents, and my great Benefactor and Redeemer? If these be inconsistent with each other, and sinful in the person with whom they exist together, I am in an awful dilemma. For the first I will not, the second I cannot, and the last I ought not, must not, cease to love."

"Love is a generic name, comprising under it many distinct species and might with propriety have so many different names. Love between the sexes, filial love, and love of a benefactor are three species of the Genus love. It was the indivisibility of the species of which I spoke. Him who died to save us we may love with all our hearts, — our parents we may love perfectly, a person of the opposite sex, and only one, we may love sincerely and passionately. Besides these you may, in a vague sense which none but divines can explain, love all human kind."

Belinda thanked him for this elucidation of the term; but said there was no occasion for using argument with her as to the fate of the letter in her hand, or in respect to Van Corts as he was a man whom she always did detest. Then throwing her arm around the neck of Rowland and touching her lips to his she rose and threw the letter behind the grate. This was the omega of poor Van Corts and he went the way of Barnabas the Jew!

"Now," said Fitz Rowland, "I *know* that you love me, and look forward with confidence to the time when we shall enjoy each other without any expectation of parting."

"I hope that will be very soon, Rowland," replies Belinda, "for although I feel a very strong attachment for my present home, yet would I very gladly exchange it for one, with you, in the torrid or the frigid zone."

"I do not know your father and mother's mind toward me, or whether they would consent that I should take from them a daughter whom I know they love tenderly and without dissimulation."

"Here are paper, pen and ink, address a note to them at once. I'm confident they will not refuse any thing upon which my happiness for life depends."

"I will, my own Belinda; you never looked so beautiful as you do now; I never loved you more. My love is without satiety — it never can pall. It never can diminish or grow cold." Rowland took a sheet of gold-edged paper and, with a trembling hand, wrote the subjoined:

"Clifton Hall, May 17th, 1833.

"Dear Sir and Madam — I shall abruptly introduce the subject of this note, by saying that I sincerely love your fair daughter, Belinda. She professes the same affectionate regard for me, and has consented, with your concurrence, to become the partner of my future good and ill.

"I humbly beg the privilege of blessing her with all that I possess, and by every means within my power. I very respectfully solicit that you will let me understand the conclusion of your deliberations, by dropping me a line.

"Your most dutiful, most humble serv't,

"N. Fitz Rowland."

"J. Howard,
"M. Howard."

In reply to the above, the following was immediately returned:

"Clifton Hall, May 17th, 1833.

"Dear Sir — We have this moment read your agreeable note, and take great pleasure in saying, that you have our unqualified permission to make Belinda yours forever. We have entire confidence in the judgment of our daughter, in her ability to choose for herself; and we would be but ill consulting her future happiness, by thwarting her in the choice she has made.

"Affectionately yours,

"J. Howard,
"M. Howard."

"Mr. N. Fitz Rowland."

When this flattering answer was known, Belinda, as she sat with her head reclined upon the breast of Rowland, said, with great earnestness, "I am now, just where, and what, and who, I wish to be. I would not exchange my present hopes, and situation by your side, for the princess Victoria's prospect of a throne. With her confined, imprisoned love, every interested lord and lawyer in the realm, will be tampering, until she be persuaded to bestow her hand upon some false Frenchman, spiteful Spaniard, or doubting Dutchman. Whenever she moves abroad, a score of cringing miscreants forms her train, and at every turn she is greeted with the loud huzzas of an unthinking mob. But I am happier, far. I have one, who says he loves me, one who means what he says, one between whom and me, there is no insurmountable barrier. My name is not Howard now, but Rowland. This bleak, and by boreas, blasted shore is not my home. There is a valley in the west, a garden like the one called paradise, where I am destined, by the bounteous and gracious hand which wisely orders all events, to spend my life with thee."

"My dear Belinda, I cannot give utterance, in suitable language, to the complete joy which now pervades the obscurest corner of my soul — and body too, if 'tis not incompatible with matter. You must not judge me for my taciturnity. I have a feeling heart, but my store of words is small. When shall we celebrate our nuptials?"

"Each day we live, between this time and that, is so much real loss of life; at least of that far happier life, upon which we then shall enter. Some preparations, however, will be requisite before I can appear worthy to be your bride, among a gladsome company of friends. It will be befitting the occasion, and my father will, I know, insist upon that day's passing with considerable eclat."

"I am willing and desirous that it should, and for that purpose, have no objections to a postponement of one month."

"That will be very long — but, as you say, one month will be the time."

"Then on the seventeenth of June, you'll be my wife."

"The seventeenth of June! I wish that day were come."

Miss Howard, starting up suddenly, as if some new thought had just then entered her mind, went to her bureau, and took out the following part of a letter, saying, that as she was reading it the evening before, it accidentally came in contact with the candle, and was half consumed, before she could extinguish the blaze. "It would," said she, "be very wrong for me to keep anything secret from you, my dear Rowland. The letter is from the cashier, and if there be a single person of the race of Adam, whom I hate, it is the author of this piece of scribbleing. We are commanded to love them that hate us — what a happy thing that there is nothing in the scriptural code about loving them that *love* us. Swift may boast of his having kept the law, with a very good grace; for I am sure, that if he loves me, he loves *one* who hates him with a perfect hatred. Though, 'tis true, he has not spoken to me, nor I to him, since I left my uncle's in the valley."

yourself,
to expedite the
as ever, nor shall I
can have no cause to repent,
nd is unchanged; then shall we
infinitely more than any other person,
because you, no doubt, have frequently,
; and are at present in possession of at least one. Though, I must confess, I was partly influenced in taking up my pen, by the confident expectation of receiving something at your hands, which would yield me some permanent, personal advantage, yet the motive that induces me to address you, is not altogether a sinister one. It will, I flatter myself, if the proposal be accepted, be adding to *your* happiness, increasing the pleasure of your life, and enlarging the field where you revel in enjoyments; as well as putting a termination to my present miserable state of suspense, and raising me to a state of bliss not much surpassed by that of *the hundred and forty-four thousand.*

"In this world and the next, may Heaven grant me a place by thy dear side.

"Your true lover,

"J.B. Swift."

Rowland examined this scrap as closely as possible, endeavored to supply what was wanting, and asked Belinda a number of questions, which showed that even then he lacked confidence in her whom he so ardently loved. He thought there might have been something in the first part of the letter, which she did not wish him to see; the cashier might have acknowledged the receipt of a note from her, or mentioned what had passed between them in conversation; and she might, in consequence, have purposely destroyed a part of it, and kept the other part, the more completely to impose upon him. Rowland silenced his fears in the best manner he was able; told Belinda there could be no harm in *re-*

ceiving a communication from any one; and walked out into the yard. Who should he see there but the very identical cashier, with whom he was made acquainted at the old Burgher's? He was a gentleman of talent, if not of solid worth; affable, easy of access, and calculated to gain the esteem even of a rival. It was now dark. Rowland, for reasons best known to himself, proposed that they should both occupy the same bed that night, to which the cashier at once consented, and complaining of fatigue, they retired early. Mack, becoming acquainted with this circumstance, requested an hour's audience for himself, which was very readily granted. What passed between them that night, is known only to Him, who causeth thunder, and I shall not pretend to divulge it. It would seem, however, from the subsequent conduct of the Scotchman, that an agreement had about this time been entered into, between him and Belinda, to this effect — that when there was no other person in waiting, preferable to himself, he should, at his pleasure, have the freedom of her company. But, if any respectable young gentleman should appear, then he (McLeod,) was to keep his distance. Accordingly, he never afterwards seemed to regard her conduct with the same jealous eye. He even assisted her in duping others, thinking, thereby, to insinuate himself into her favor, and gain upon her uncertain affection. Wary as he was the storm proved his foundation sand.

As might be expected Rowland and the Cashier had not been long in company before the conversation turned upon Esq. Howard's beautiful daughter.

"What do you think of her," says Swift, "in downright earnest? — She is handsome, no question, but is she, in every respect, faultless?"

"If she has any imperfections about her — any flaws in her character, or foibles in her disposition, they are to my eyes and senses lost amidst the multiplicity of her beauties and virtues."

"That is, (to be ingenuous,) exactly my opinion of the young lady; but as I am in love with her I ought to suspect the correctness of any impressions which I may receive through the medium of my senses and be governed, if possible, by reason. But philosophers have attempted to prove that lovers have no reason, and I half believe that some of these unreasonable reasoners reason well! I thought you were in your right mind, and would for a few moments be neighborly and lend me your reason, but I now perceive that you are but little better, if any, than myself!"

"I will be as frank with you as you have been with me. I am Belinda's lover too; and more than that she loves me in return. She has consented to become my wife, her parents have agreed to the union and the day itself is named!"

"Say no more, Fitz Rowland, say no more." The next morning the poor frantic Cashier as a last effort sent the under-written note by the hands of her brother to Miss Howard.

May 18th, 1833.

Fair Belinda — If you have forsaken me at last, as seems from what I've heard to be the case, all I ask is that you will let me know the cause? I pray you let me hear it from your lips, and you will

Oblige a broken-hearted lover,

Swift.

Belinda bit her lips when she read this, but seeing no alternative, wrote on the same piece of paper these words, "the prayer of the petition is not granted," and sent it directly back. When the Cashier received his doom he said it was the first time ever he had failed in an endeavor to take gold from the bullion and change it to coin; then bolted from the house as if the hottest fiend below had been, with all his instruments of torture, hard at his heels.

Fitz Rowland had now no further obstacle to surmount, no equal in the field, none worthy of the name of a rival to oppose him. At the breakfast table he sat next Belinda, in the place of the (as he supposed) crest fallen Mack, who took a lower seat that he might unobserved sap the enemy's walls.

With renewed professions of invariable love and confidence, Rowland and Belinda parted, to meet again before the seventeenth of June. Rowland, as he rode along, could not help secretly congratulating himself upon his success, where so many had failed. He was now positively sure of the prize. Nothing but death could intervene. That she should yet decline his hand, or prove unworthy, was utterly impossible. And then she was so fair in her person, so amiable in her disposition, so intellectual in her mind, and so religious in her conduct.

There never was a man so base as not to prefer a pious wife. But, know all men by these presents, that I do not mean he would choose, as a help meet, one who might preach a sermon twice a day. Preachment, and piety are not often, perhaps never, found together in a woman. The very act of females publicly declaiming, even upon the subject of religion, as Belinda sometimes did, is diametrically opposed to many plain injunctions in the book which they would recommend, and therefore wrong. There is not one example of high authority and great success to be found in any age or nation, we therefore may presume it to be wrong. It is leaving the station to which she was at first appointed, throwing off all her native grace, and usurping the office of another better qualified to perform its duties than she — it is therefore wrong. Why, "even reason teaches us it is a shame unto her." It is disgusting to beholders, and condemned by the common sense, and common assent of mankind generally. I only recollect one female preacher noticed in the New Testament, but St. Paul had no sooner commanded the *familiar spirit* to come out of her, than she ceased preaching. By a "pious wife," I meant not one who says she is, *but one who is a really good woman.* I was drawn insensibly into this digression, by my love, I hope, rather than by my hatred of the fair.

At the Clifton Hall no mean preparations were making for the wedding, for Esq. Howard was not only highly pleased with the connection his daughter was about forming, but he valued his own reputation, and was anxious that every thing which was to be presented to the view, or offered to the taste of the guests, should strike them at once by its superior qualities, as something uncommon or rare. Partly to accomplish this object, by purchasing whatever was either curious or useful, and partly for the health of Miss Sophia, a younger sister of Belinda's, (a good girl, and far above being either pleased or profited by any panegyric from my pen,) who, together with her mother, accompanied him, he took a tour to the east, expecting to be from home two or three weeks. An undue confidence in Belinda, caused any precaution for her safety, to be quite unthought of. As for Mack, he had free egress to the Hall, or to any part of it, at any hour, which might suit his own convenience; although Brock and he were at this time by no means intimate friends.

While her parents were absent, Miss Howard was very frequently in the company of her aunt Howard, who, I am sorry to say, was almost an equal for the lady of the old Burgher. She had all the functions of a gossip in perfection — a bigoted sectarian, a profound party politician, and a general supervisor of other people's concerns. The very three qualifications, which, above all others, I most religiously despise in a woman. I see no reason why a female may not be strongly attached to any particular form of church, or even State government; but a charitable disposition towards those who differ with her in opinion, can never appear unlovely. Perhaps I shall be thought singular, but it appears to me that she *may* wish well to her neighbors, without diving into all their secrets, for the purpose of publishing the minutest faults of each. My intention, however, when I commenced writing, was to *give every dog his due* to tell what certain characters actually were, rather than what they ought to have been, and to leave all to exercise their own judgments, and draw their own inferences.

One day, about a week after Esq. Howard, with his lady and daughter had left home, Belinda invited her aunt to drink a cup of tea with her. They were no sooner together, than the proposed marriage of her *dear niece*, with Fitz Rowland, was brought up by Mrs. Howard, as a fruitful theme for conversation. She descanted at considerable length, upon the depravity of men in general, and the little confidence which should be placed in their professions; the gaiety and agreeableness of frippery and flirtation, while one remained single; and the dull monotony, and cramped vexatiousness of a married life. "Of course," says she, arching her brows still higher, and taking her cup in one hand, and her saucer in the other, "of course, the idea of dying an old maid, of dying without having done something towards populating the world, of dying without any reason, to believe that your name will be remembered by a future generation; of course, such thoughts as these, are not altogether pleasant."

"Why then you have raised a strong argument in favor of my proceeding in my agreement with Rowland, which indeed I feel an inclination to fulfil."

"Nonsense; you could not possibly take a more foolish or ill-advised step at present. You are not yet twenty years old, have a beautiful face, and half a dozen beaux, and afraid of being an old maid, unless you jump at the first chance, and grasp the first fool that comes within your reach!"

"But, my dear aunt, I am positively engaged."

"Engaged! well what of that? What do men care for an engagement? — not one straw. It binds them like the green withs with which the Philistines bound Samson. They answered an admirable purpose while he pleased to lie still. But when he determined to go what boot, bonds, promises, or wife? They are the stronger, we the weaker sex. They are able to defend themselves from all that we can do in any other way than this; but here they are sometimes in our power, and it is right, I ween, and just, to make them feel it."

"A person must injure us before we can wish for vengeance. — Rowland has never injured me, nor have I any sufficient reason for believing such to be his intention."

"Well done! Belinda is in love! She has fallen deep in love with an unprepossessing and suspicious looking stranger. We may and ought to wish for vengeance — and to take it too — upon those who have not injured us individually, if the sex, sect, party, or nation to which they belong have inflicted any wrong upon the sex, sect, party, or nation which we represent or to which we belong. Carry out the principle which you have laid down, and see how it will work. — When our country was invaded by banditti from the greatest republic in the world — the inhabitants on the frontier murdered and their dwellings reduced to ashes — according to your reasoning those in the interior ought not to have moved one finger to oppose them, until the instruments of death glistened before their own eyes, or touched their own heart-strings."

"Your reasoning in favor of war under particular circumstances, — though I am not like you skilled in civil polity, — appears conclusive enough, but candidly I do not perceive its applicability to the question before us."

"Well, I ought not to have used the simile; I ought to have known that a lover cannot understand the plainest language, much less that which is embellished with tropes and figures. But if you are not incorrigible you shall know my meaning now. Fitz Rowland has not lived so long and never been loved before. He has, like other men, I will venture to say, deceived and deserted many of our too credulous, too relying, and too charitable sex. And what security have you that you shall be more fortunate than others have been? none at all. Be before-hand with him then. It is a credit to a young lady to have it said that she has rejected forty-nine, but a great disgrace to be cast off herself by one. Though Rowland deserves not your love, yet if you are absolutely crazy for a husband; and if you are willing to run the awful risk of trusting him; and if he happen (for the chances are against you) to prefer you to many others for a wife — a slave, — then marry him; but talk not of being bound by engagements! That shows your inexperience. You are as free as any bird that flits the air. See that gold-finch through the window — there it is gone! Would it be happier in a cage?"

"If I decline this offer and shrink back after having advanced so far, Rowland will be annoyed, no doubt, and suffer by the act; but the more I think of it the more dreadful is my fear of just retribution even in this life; something whispers me my vengence shall react with redoubled force upon my own devoted head!"

"Superstitious too! as well as love sick! another striking likeness of Cleopatra. Here is an onion now, fall on your knees! The little, white, rotund divinity consult, and learn from it how you should act."

"I do not believe in vegetable gods, nor is my brain disordered yet with love — but there is a God in heaven, him I fear. What you now advise me to, I need not tell you, has often — too often for my good name — been done by me already. I feel, just now, more like Caesar on the banks of the Rubicon than like Cleopatra. It is, today, in my power to save myself and friends from a perdurable shame, to-morrow the die may be cast — I hesitate and am unresolved."

"For my part, if you will pardon me Belinda, I would a thousand times rather stand at the side of the jolly Mack and vow to stick there till I died than to become the wife of the grum and guileful Fitz. — Besides you may spend five years if you please yet in playing with the Scotchman, and then not marry him after all. But young enough, still have your choice of half a score of extended hands."

"If I were sure of this it would go far in enabling me to come to a decision. I really like, if not love, the affable and laughing Mack, and as for Rowland, upon my word I hope that he loves me better than I do him."

"You have no sufficient grounds for your hope, but from what has come to my knowledge, I am very well satisfied, that what love there is between you is principally on your side. Now, Belinda, take advice; when Rowland comes (if he ever do come) let him see at once, by your conduct, that you do not love him; and if he ask you what the matter is — answer angrily that you wish he would not meddle with what concerns not him."

"What will my parents say when they hear of this? They think all the world of Rowland, besides, their consent has been asked and obtained. This is what puzzles me."

"You would marry then to please your parents! This is the practise in some pagan countries, but christians ought to, and generally do, know better."

"If by pleasing them I enhance my own happiness it will be no slur upon the christian name."

"Well, I will say no more — but hope, when you again meet him to whom you're chained, you'll think of what your aunt has said, and make one desperate struggle to get free!"

The very next afternoon, Belinda received a note, respectfully requesting the favor of her company, at the house of her uncle Howard. This note, purporting to be from her aunt, Brock, who insisted upon seeing it, knew to be in the hand writing of McLeod. Nothing could have been more indisputable evidence of the strict intimacy existing between the trio — and Brock was wonderfully excited about a thing of no kind of consequence. The invitation was accepted, in defiance of the remonstrances of her brother, "always frightened," as she declared, "by far-fancied ills and dangers out of sight." Miss Howard, staying later that evening than usual, McLeod, quite innocently, walked over to accompany her home — but Brock, suspecting that all was not right, and that a secret conspiracy was being formed, prejudicial to the interests of his friend Rowland, and disgraceful to his father's family, thought proper to see his sister home that night himself. When he went in at his uncles, his aunt, Belinda, and Mack were sitting very near each other, and apparently occupied in something of intense interest. He rather roughly made his business known, and with his hat in his hand, refused to be seated.

"I will go when I get ready," retorted his sister; "I'm not afraid of ghosts, you need not wait."

Brock. "No, you are not afraid to sit there, in a fraternity of incarnate devils. But I'm peremptory, come take my arm."

Mrs. H. "Peremptory! Then I peremptorily tell you to leave the room."

Belinda. "I decline accepting your offered assistance, Brock."

Brock: "I shall leave this room very soon, aunt, but not be blown away by a breath of wind — and as for you, Belinda, you are too much accustomed to the use of that word 'decline;' you decline every thing which would be for your own, or your friends' advantage — you are declining far and fast from the path of virtue and respectability, and dragging others with you, down the dread declivity to undeserved disparagement. But I'm *commanding* now, not *courting*, and must be obeyed."

Mack. "I feel myself insulted by your words and conduct, Brock."

Brock. "Silence! thou scurrilous, foul-mouthed villain. If you but interpose another word, then let them who value their own safety not stand between me and the object of my wrath!"

Mrs. Howard poured her *sincere blessings* on the head of Brock, while he, placing Belinda's bonnet on her head, and taking her by the hand, proved himself the stronger of the two. They *lovingly* walked home together, and Mack went to his lodgings.

CHAPTER V.

Belinda, like Eve, had listened with pleasure to the voice of the temptor, if not eaten of the fruit, and was now walking her room, seriously deliberating how she should act. She had notice from Fitz Rowland that he still loved her dearly, and might be expected on the fifth of June to visit the Clifton Hall. That day had now arrived. A war of the elements of life was furiously carried on within her breast — her bosom heaved and swelled with the ferment. It was the last effort of expiring virtue! She was soon cool, and resolved what to do. Her hair was disheveled — she dressed herself like a slattern, so as scarcely to appear decent — spoiled her face with ugly frowns, put on as unlovely a mien as could be manufactured for the occasion, and went down stairs. Rowland rode into the yard where Brock was standing, to give him a hearty welcome. He turned his eyes towards the house, expecting, at least, to see Belinda's smiling face at the window. It did not appear, and he asked Brock if his sister was at home and well. He was answered in the affirmative, and they walked in together. As soon as the door was opened, Rowland was thunderstruck, (and even Brock was astonished,) at the ridiculous plight in which Miss Howard appeared as she sat at the other end of the room. He felt as if he had entered a charnel house, and every chair and table was a ghost, and his own sighs, and those of poor Brock, were the groans of expiration. "Belinda," said Rowland, when he had with cautious step, approached her — the hair rising on his head and his voice faltering, "I hope you have not forgotten me — I love you still." Then taking her by the hand, while she contracted the nerves of her arm, he asked her plainly if she loved him not. That tongue, which had been so often praised as more fit for an angel than a mortal, replied, after a sullen pause, "No! I never loved you." He quickly let fall her hand, and stepped back. He felt as if he had touched some putrifying corpse, which benumbed his flesh and chilled the blood within his veins. He folded his arms across his breast, and there, pale and stiff, stood like a statue! or like some tall forester, some monarch of the woods, which, but one moment before, was flourishing in all its pride of power and of place, and looking down on them which stood around; not blasted by a sudden stroke of electric fire, its haughty head brought low, and all its luxuriant ornaments of fluttering leaves, with boughs and branches, scattered to the winds. Rowland, again recovering from the stupefaction of his amazement, said, "do you not recollect, Belinda, the promises which were to be fulfilled on the seventeenth of this present month?"

"I've changed my mind," returns Belinda, raising her voice to the highest pitch, "since last I saw your odious and abhorrent phiz, and have determined never to marry the man I cannot love."

"But surely, I am not the man, Belinda, whom you cannot love, and therefore will not marry!"

"You are the man; I love you not. Is that plain enough?"

"Quite plain enough! But do your father and mother, and Miss Sophia know of this? What will they say?"

"How would they, you miserable dolt, be acquainted with a circumstance which occurred just now, and they two hundred miles from home! I care not, at the least, what my sister says or thinks. And as for my parents, it is my concern, not yours, to make my peace with them. You need not catechise me any further. I will not answer you another question; but hope you will be satisfied that I never loved you — never will!"

"Good by, Belinda, and more than that, good by forever."

Brock almost bursting with rage and meditating direful revenge, followed Rowland out. He knew not which to blame the most or where first to strike the blow. Like a man bereft of his reason he talked at random, loading his sister, his aunt, and Mack with maledictions; and applying to them, and the act of which they had been guilty, every opprobrious epithet which his cultivated, and infuriated, genius could invent. And had it not been for the meditation of Rowland I am apprehensive that some who were then in full health and spirits might not have seen the sun go down that night. Rowland went with Brock to his own rooms, wrote the following hasty and incoherent letter to Esq. Howard, and gave it to Brock to hand his father when he came home.

Clifton Hall, June 5th, 1833.

Dear Sir' — I write this oppressed with sorrow and covered with shame. Your daughter, Belinda, at a very late stage of the contract, has absolutely refused any terms; rejected all proposals for a coalition; disgraced you, and ruined me. I thought her beautiful exterior had been but a prelude to the more excellent qualities of her mind. Alas, "all is not gold that glitters." Fool that I was! Because the brass was bright to take it for the precious metal. I call myself a fool — others may spare me if they please. I am greatly obliged to Brock. I shall not pretend to say how much I feel indebted to yourself — my dutiful respects to Mrs. Howard. My esteem to Miss Sophia. Respectfully your humble ser't.,

N. Fitz Rowland

J. Howard, Esq.

CHAPTER VI

"O, mischief, thou art swift
To enter in the thoughts of desperate men.
I do remember an apothecary,
And in his needy shop a tortoise hung,
An alligator stuffed, and other skins
Of ill-shaped fishes; and about his shelves
A beggarly account of empty boxes.
Noting this penury, to myself I said,
An if a man did need a poison now,
Here lives a caitiff wretch would sell it him."

Fitz Rowland determined not to outlive his disgrace, bid his friend Brock good by, went to an apothecary's shop and bought of the *"caitiff wretch"* a bottle of laudanum! Clouds as black as the smoke of a pit obscured the western and north-western sky; the lightning was darting terrifically along the vault; and, now and then, the solid earth itself was shaken by a discharge of heaven's heaviest artillery. Rowland's horse, a half-blood Arabian, stood at the gate, saddled and bridled, pawing the ground and champing the bits, with his nostrils extended wide and his eyes sparkling fire. He mounted him, gave him the rein, and like a ball fresh from the cannon's mouth, he was on his way, he knew not — cared not whither.

The shades of night were gathering round; the fury of the storm was beginning to subside; the distant thunder, at intervals, still bellowing as it retired, like some brave corps after a disastrous battle, as Fitz Rowland entered a dense wood about two leagues from the Clifton Hall. He dismounted, tied his lathered steed to a sapling, and, as he walked slowly on, ruminating upon the desperate alternative to which he was driven, took out and uncorked his vial of opiates, hoping that, by taking them, he might procure to himself that eternal sleep of forgetfulness for which he languished.

With a heavy sigh he sat down with his back against the trunk of a spreading oak. That was an awful moment! His agitated nerves relaxed — became powerless, and neglected to obey the call of his unflinching will. His hand, holding the deadly liquid, rested upon his knee, and refused its needed aid to the most horrid act of suicide. — Thought, imperishable thought, began to return; reason again resumed its lofty seat, and he, after a long pause and much perturbation, began the following soliloquy:

"By tossing off this easy, dreadful draught, I shall forget at once my love and hate — shall save myself from meeting the reproachful laugh of those who never felt the pangs of disappointment, and sink my name at once into oblivion. My worthless, unthinking and unfeeling carcase here, will lie guarded by the waking owl till morn, unless, perchance, some ravenous wolf give it fit sepulture within his famished maw before that time. But, when I cease to breathe, is it quite certain that I shall lose all knowledge of myself and others? Matter, from its very nature, cannot think; and though my body lose its power of locomotion, and cease to be the receptacle of a soul, yet, I sadly fear, that thinking part will still exist. It may dart, in one short second, beyond the planet Herschel, and there, in even less indulgent climes than these, brood over its misfortunes and think of Belinda, so fair and so false. * * * This world is all one bleak desert, without a single spot of fertile, pleasureable ground to rest the tired view. * * * I stand upon the brink of an awful precipice, where there is nought about me I can love, or that might make me content to live among these crags and rocks. But, when I look below, my brains begin to swim. I instinctively shrink back, and hesitate to take the desperate plunge. If I, with certainty, could leap at once into annihilation, I would not hesitate one moment, but with a laughing countenance and a glad heart, would cast myself down headlong. * * * But what if the bible should prove true, (and something like a whisper from the depths profound seems just now to tell me that it will,) my circumstances would not be improved! Well, I will yet a while endure my present miseries — the thoughts of my inestimable loss — the caprice of the changeable — the contumely of the proud — rather than plunge myself at once into interminable wo!"

Then, as if offering a libation to some deity, he slowly poured the cursed distillation on the ground, thanked the God of heaven that he was yet alive, and, with a somewhat lighter heart, re-mounted his Arabian. It was not because he was tenacious of life, nor because he thought there remained any thing in this world worth the trouble of gaining, but because he was afraid to die that he had consented to live.

When Fitz Rowland arrived at his own home, his blood-shot eyes and wobegone appearance could not be mistaken. His mother and sisters read the tale in his face ere it was told. They were not sorry of the occurrence — told him it was for his ultimate good, and even went so far as to say they believed it to be one of the most fortunate and happy events which had ever been ordered by a beneficent Providence for his real welfare. This was a kind of language which he did not understand. These were arguments which he was not prepared to appreciate. It might, he doubted not, have happened under the direction or superintendence of the wise hand of Providence, but that did not better the thing itself. It only made his present condition appear the more terrific, as he could not look upon it in any other light, than that of a terrible judgment. He said he was now driven out to walk the earth alone, like a vagabond all his life. He retired to a private room, and, forgetting all he ever had read, of the philosophy of the stoics, and that a little of it, though perhaps too stern a virtue for a woman, is at all times becoming in a man — threw himself across the very bed, on which the love-sick Belinda once had laid, and wept aloud. Here we shall at present leave him, and on the rapid wings of thought, fly back to the Clifton Hall. Brock had not given up his intention of making them who had, as he thought, very greatly disparaged his father's family, feel the weight of his arm. He declared himself master of the house, and forbid Mack, at the peril of his existence, from placing his cloven foot upon the threshold of the outside door. He sent a polite note to his aunt, requesting her not to endanger her own safety by trespassing upon the premises connected with the Clifton Hall, and kept a secret eye upon all the motions of his sister.

In spite of the vigilance of Brock, in spite of his threats, in spite of the dictates of common decency, Belinda was one day known to carry a plum pudding to Mack at his lodgings, and to stay long enough to help him eat it. Brock was now roused, and ripe for the most desperate adventure, and only waited for a favorable opportunity of striking with certainty and effect. This was not long wanting.

Not many days after the flight of Fitz Rowland, while Brock was in a distant field, happening to ascend a rising ground and turning his eyes towards the Hall, he saw a gentleman enter the door, and from his quickstep instantly suspected Mack. He immediately chose one of the most active and courageous men which were with him as an accomplice; but not so much for the assistance which he expected to need from him as that he might have him as an evidence of what passed, or to corroborate what himself should say, if the affair should ever be brought before a court of justice. Brock and Bastino hastily armed themselves with cudgels, took a circuitous route, and that they might not be observed, approached from an opposite quarter. Had McLeod been advised of this in time he would like Sir John Falstaff, upon a somewhat similar occasion, have gladly consented to be stuffed into a buckbasket among foul linnen and greasy nightcaps, and conveyed — to bedlam or any place else that he might have avoided a battle with unequal numbers and under circumstances so unfavorable. The enemy were within the gate before they were seen. It was too late to think of escape. Belinda was frightened into a fit of the hysterics. The conduct of Mack was worthy of a better cause. He did not for a moment lose his presence of mind, nor neglect the means of defending himself in his apparently hopeless situation. The only means of defence within his reach was a short cutlass, which he, for two or three days, contrary to his usual custom, and without the knowledge of Brock, had carried with him. This he unsheathed and stood prepared; and determined if his life were taken it should be at a valuation. Brock and Bastino rushed up stairs, but they were a little surprised at the posture in which they found Mack. They expected to see him on his knees praying for mercy, instead of which he stood with a sword drawn over his shoulder and impudently offering, if he were not molested, peaceably to leave the house. To this they replied that he had nothing to do but to lay down his arms and surrender at discretion; no terms could be granted — no lenient usage must be expected.

"Ruffians and cut-throats!" cries Mack, "I know right well that to surrender to such as you were instant death, and to lay down my arms were to lay down my life. But I have too much confidence in this, my trusty sword, to yield without a trial to dispair; and cringe to the commonest black-guards."

"One stroke of my good white-oak cudgel," says Bastino coolly, "will change your metre, and you'll sing another tune."

"There is no time for parley," adds Brock, "have at him."

They closed upon him; but every blow from their sticks of wood was dexterously met and fended off. Like lightning above his head, on every side and on all sides at once the shining cutlass flew. The enemy gave ground. Mack followed up his advantage, and at last down stairs he darted, like Satan when he fell from heaven, and a storm of clubs and chairs and broken furniture precipitately followed. Mack fled from the house a little bruised, 'tis true, but not seriously injured. This was the last time ever Mack, the Scotchman, saw the interior of the Clifton Hall; and Belinda was left without a lover and almost without a friend!

Brock now turned his grim visage towards his sister, who was just beginning to revive from the languor of her paroxysm. She asked him if he had come to murder her in her own room, and if Bastino had already killed Mr. McLeod? He answered, "you have already destroyed your own life, and half a dozen others, by your infamous conduct; or what is the same thing, put an end to the agreeableness of living, by loading all to whom you are related, with everlasting disgrace. I had no intention of striking you; but inquire no farther what has become of Mack, lest I lose all self-command, and do what I should afterwards be sorry for. You will, I foresee, receive condign punishment in the fortune of your future life, and that must be greater, and more severe, than I could wish to see inflicted upon any poor degraded human being of your sex. And now, Belinda, you have driven me forever from the country of my birth and choice, from my friends and home. I will not stay to be pointed at, as I pass along the street, and hear it said, 'there goes the brother of the false Belinda.' I straight will pass the frontiers of a Province, over which a sceptre's swayed — a sceptre which I love. I'll leave the safe retreat between the lion's paws, and seek protection from the eagle's spreading wings and crooked beak. Say not a word, Belinda. I do not wish to hear you speak. Adieu."

Brock did not leave home immediately, but determined upon doing so as soon as his father returned. Time dragged heavily. The Clifton Hall had the appearance of some old castle, from which the inhabitants had been frighted by ghosts and apparitions. No laughing groups of the young and innocent were seen in the yard. No strangers passing in and out. The measured step of the melancholy Brock sounded along the hall; and the pale, but still beautiful face of the repenting Belinda, might, ever and anon, be seen, as she wistfully looked from her chamber window. On the twelfth of June, the return of Esq. Howard was announced. The news struck Belinda dumb. She saw the carriage drive into the yard, and sank down upon the sofa, not daring to go out to meet his incensed look, or the chidings of her mother. The news had reached them two days' ride from home. Sophia was deeply affected by the report. She said she would much rather, although she loved Belinda well, but she would much rather have heard that her sister was dead, than that she had gone so far, and then had retracted from so many solemn promises. Her mother hoped that it was not true, or that more than the truth had been told. She hoped there were many extenuating circumstances, which, in a correct recital, would make it appear much less ignominious. Sophia feared the reverse — she apprehended that truth would rather aggravate than mitigate the crime, and its disgrace.

When they had come into the house, and heard the whole story from Brock, without palliation in one part, or reserve in another; and when the letter from Fitz Rowland had been read, there was no more room for disbelieving. Sophia had gone up stairs, and in the kindest manner possible, after the mutual greetings had passed, requested her sister to come down. She still hesitated, but at last consented. As soon as she saw her mother, who sat weeping, she flew across the room, clasped her arms around her neck, and kissed her. Mrs. Howard, taking her handkerchief from her scalded eyes, and looking affectionately up, said "Belinda, my dear Belinda, you have broken my heart!" Offering to salute her father, he unfeelingly pushed her back, and sternly ordered a servant to bring him his horse whip.

Belinda fell upon her knees and begged his pardon. She had heard of Rowland, what she now believed to be false. She had been overpersuaded by her aunt Howard, and, in an unlucky moment, thinking it would be for the best, had refused to be bound by her engagement.

"I disown you — you are not my child," said Esq. Howard. "You have involved us all in ruin and disgrace, and from this time shall live by begging, and eat the bread of charity. Begone from my sight, thou monster!"

"My dear, dear father," replied Belinda, "your words are more than I can bear. Your anger, though just, is more than I can long endure. You need not strike me; — a few more such harsh and harrowing expressions will frighten me to death, and save you the thoughts — uncomfortable, perhaps, in future — of having slain, with violent hands, or banished, your own daughter. I will not leave your feet until you pardon me, unless, by the hair of my aching head, my father, you should drag me forth and lay me in the street."

"My dear husband," said Mrs. Howard, "your excited feelings carry you beyond all bounds. Have you no natural affection left? No compassion for one, our own daughter, who seeks it carefully with tears? Remember, that only those who show mercy can expect it in their turn, when they come to sue for it before a higher Judge, where the only plea which any of us can have, will be, that we are sorry that we have offended, without the possibility of making the smallest restitution."

Belinda, who still continued on her knees, her hair hanging over her face, and the tears running down her cheeks, said — "I am sincerely sorry for what has happened, and would most gladly, if it were within my power, regain what I have lost."

"Will you consent," asked her father, "to write this afternoon a letter to Fitz Rowland, begging his pardon and respectfully inviting him to return?"

"I will, with confidence that he will yet accept me."

"That will be adding insult to injury," grumbles Brock, "and you may expect to be insulted with a vengeance in return."

"Go to your room, Belinda," said her father; "prepare your letter, and, ere the sun goes down, bring it to me. I also will write. — I feel in hopes all may yet be well."

"I thank you, father," replied Belinda, "for these words so kind."

Belinda, with feelings at which I shall not pretend to guess, for fear that I should do her an injustice, soon penned the following:

"Clifton Hall, June 12th, 1833.
"My Dear and Much-injured Rowland:

"After the most unfortunate conversation which took place between us on the fifth instant, can you pardon me for presuming to address you by this fond title? Oh! how I wish that I could recall that unhappy day, and live it over again! The unkind words which escaped my lips, still ring like death bells in my ears. Did I say that I never loved you — never would? It seems to me like an indistinct recollection of some horrible — most horrible and frightful dream! If it were not that Brock remembers all the unhappy incidents of that dark day, I would persuade myself that I have been deceived by a vision, and that you, the only one on earth who ever had possession of my whole soul, had not appeared since the glad seventeenth of May.

"*I never loved you — never will!*" Gracious heaven! I am undone. Those words came not from my heart. They were the vagaries of a heated brain, which soon was cool. Yes, my dearest Rowland, I hope you will believe that my tongue, on that occasion, belied my heart. I did — do, and always will love you, and only you. Many things were told me, to which I was guilty for listening. I thought — fatal thought! I thought it prudent not to be too hasty in doing a thing which can never be undone. I do not know how I came to speak so harshly and so positively; but the most distant idea of giving you up altogether, never entered my head. No — nothing could be farther from my thoughts. That would be to deprive myself of all the happiness which I expect to enjoy in this life, and if that must be the case, I shall be induced to take the veil in some Romish convent, and quit all intercourse with men.

"Oh, the unfortunate fifth of June! The thoughts of that unhappy day will kill me yet, unless you pardon me and love me as you did before. My heart, my heart is breaking! Forgive me — I can hold my pen no longer! I can write no more! Do you not love me, Rowland? My life depends upon the answer you shall make.

"Your unworthy but sincere lover,

"Belinda."

The underwritten is the letter of Esq. Howard, whose zeal, methinks, was, at that time, not altogether "according to knowledge."

"Clifton Hall, June 12th, 1833.

"My very Dear Sir:

"I have received yours of the fifth, and feel the full weight of your remark when you say that *Belinda has ruined you and disgraced me.* The news reached us many miles from home. Mrs. Howard, judging from Belinda's former unblemished name and irreproachable conduct, thought the report should not be believed without the testimony of some person of known veracity.

"Sophia's appearance was that of a person in the deepest grief; so much so as to excite the attention of strangers at the hotels where we put up. She refused to take the least nourishment, and, from the effects of the anxiety of her mind, became really unwell in body by the time we arrived at home. We found Belinda sincerely sorry for what had passed, and willing and anxious to make any acknowledgment which might be thought necessary or proper; or any sacrifice of her own feelings, which might possibly lead to an amicable adjustment of the differences between herself and you. She has been imposed upon by foul reports, circulated by those who make it their constant practice to flatter the person spoken to, and slander him who is spoken of; and this, often, without the slightest acquaintance with either party.

"Belinda is now convinced that what was told her, prejudicial to your character, is utterly false. You have consequently regained your place in her affections, and again become the only object of her desires. This being the case, I see no insurmountable difficulty to prevent us from obviating the *ruin* and *disgrace* of which you speak. Mrs. Howard and myself look upon you as our own son, and feel anxious to do every thing in our power to bring about a reconciliation, and thereby to wipe out what must otherwise prove an indelible stain upon the reputation of our daughter. We shall be very happy to have you visit us as soon as convenient. You will receive a letter from Belinda, with this from her oppressed father, and I have no reason to doubt that her words precisely convey her thoughts and intentions.

"I hope you will believe me affectionately yours,

"J. Howard.

"N. Fitz Rowland, Esq."

These letters were mailed that same evening, and order and kindly feeling were restored at the Clifton Hall. Esq. Howard, feeling himself greatly injured by his brother's wife, whom he thought more guilty than she really was, imprudently determined to have it out in words. With this intent, he made his way directly to the house, and charged her with having inflicted an irremediable wound upon the honor of his family. I shall not pretend to give even the purport of what passed between them upon that occasion. For, although I have practised stenography a little, yet where two meet for the express purpose of recriminating each other; where both talk at the same time, and with all their mights; and, above all, where one of them is a woman, skilled in the profession, I find it quite impracticable to report with any approach to precision. Suffice it to say, that one talked the louder, the other the faster, and Esq. Howard returned, without having received that satisfaction which he so unreasonably expected. Nothing farther, worthy of note, occurred until the twenty second, when the subjoined letter, from Fitz Rowland, came to hand. It was dated

"Peach Grove Cottage, June 17th, 1833.

"Dear Sir — I am this moment in receipt of your very kind and flattering letter of the twelfth instant, and also of one from Belinda, bearing the same date. This is the day which was appointed for the wedding. The hour has already passed, and it has not taken place. The fault is not mine. Let them who did the injury, repair or rectify, as best they may. Once I loved Belinda, and thought that she did me. Twice she'll not deceive me. I have a modicum of sense, as well as other men, and cannot live upon a moiety of love. I shall make no other reply.

"Your most obedient,
"Most humble servant,
"N. Fitz Rowland."

"J. Howard, Esq."

This seemed to imply, that Fitz Rowland was again beginning to breathe freely the vital air. The earth, which a few days before, was all one dread desert, inhabited only by beasts of prey, was now beginning to look a little green in spots, and among the animals, some bipeds were discovered "walking with countenances erect." He perceived, with astonishment, that *the world was all before him where to choose*, and that his loss was only imaginary — or at least, a very trivial one. Indeed, a loss of this kind, if men, or women either, when the case is reversed, would only give themselves time to think, must at once vanish into nothing. If I love, I love some person, place, or thing. And that object, whatever it is, it must possess some real or fancied excellence. If real, my love, or at least my esteem, must prove permanent — if fancied, my love must expire with the discovery of the counterfeit. Now, when promises are made without a thought, and violated without a cause, to say nothing more, by any person of either sex, that person must be either of a very variable disposition, or wanting in moral truth. We need not inquire what the motive is, the act itself marks his or her place, with its diamond point, upon the scale of characters, and by looking, we shall be certain of finding it very low on that scale. This would be my antidote, this would cure me at once; and this shall prevent me from ever being greatly affected by a disappointment in love. The answer of Rowland to Esq. Howard was read before Belinda and Brock, and as the words "twice she'll not deceive me," reached their ears, he laughed, (it was not the laugh of mirth — Oh! how severe was the irony of that laugh!) said "I was only waiting for this," and immediately bid adieu to the home of his youth. She showed symptoms of fainting, and in the arms of the attendants was conveyed to her room.

When I first spoke of Esq. Howard, it was remarked that he was a *tender parent*, and I hope that has not been contradicted or falsified by his conduct towards Belinda.

He was a passionate man, naturally of a temper easily excited; but often repented having spoken as soon as the words were uttered; his treatment of his family must not, therefore, be supposed to have been in general, harsh. This was by no means the case; and Belinda might have been very happy under the paternal government and roof, had she known how to enjoy what she possessed. But she had formed to herself an ideal world of pleasure. It had just been entered, and the shadows had, one by one, faded from her view. A few days ago she was surrounded by admirers, upon whom she looked with disdain, — now she had already been reduced to the painful and shameful extremity of courting and being refused in her turn.

The five years which her aunt had advised her to spend in dazzling men's eyes, by showing herself covered with ribands and lace, and then breaking their hearts by inviting to the chase and escaping in pursuit, she now feared would not prove altogether successful, or yield her that infinitude of pleasure which had been anticipated. — She was rapidly settling down into obscurity. In company or at church, there were stupid starers without number; but they all appeared to avoid coming in close contact, as if, like the tree of knowledge of good and evil, she had been beautiful to the eye, but death to the touch. Both the Priest and Levite, when they knew that she had fallen among robbers and been very roughly handled, passed by on the other side; and even the poor Samaritan was looked for in vain. Time, in spite of lank longing melancholy, passed swiftly on. A winter and a summer came and went, and not an incident occurred worth mentioning. Belinda saw those of her own sex, whom she had so often despised, and even sometimes sympathized with on account of their *lonely condition*, rising above her one after another, and becoming agreeably and respectably settled in the world.

It may not be thought worthy of a passing observation, that Fitz Rowland, about a year after his precipitate retreat, being called by business into the neighborhood of the Clifton Hall, accidentally fell in company with Esq. Howard, and was urgently invited to his house. He excused himself in the best manner he was able, and declined accepting the invitation. Entreaties still being used, he frankly confessed his determination never again to see the face of Belinda. Even this objection was soon evaded, by a promise that she should not, without his consent, leave her room. Rowland had an inexplicable dread of the piercing, entreating, conquering eye which had once looked him through, but could not refuse so small a favor to one who appeared to regard him with so particular marks of friendship. He accordingly went to the house which, as he said, *he had seen before*, and was received by Mrs. Howard in a manner which affected him almost to tears. She told him that immediately on the receipt of his last letter, Brock left home and had never been heard from since — perhaps had committed suicide, or gone to China or the Indies; and that Belinda was quite changed — spent the greater part of her time in weeping and in devotional exercises, and still clung to him with all the fondness of earliest love. She was sure he would not hold her husband to his promise of not allowing Belinda to come into his presence. She hoped the little differences unhappily existing between them, could be very soon explained away. Rowland said he had no objections to hearing them explained away, but that his errand there that day was not to see Belinda.

"You will not — no, I am sure you cannot," said Mrs. Howard, weeping, "be so unflinchingly fixed in your mind against her, so uncomplying, so hard hearted, so insensible to the entreaties of her mother, as to object to her coming down. She will do any thing within the bounds of christianity, to atone for what has passed — she is improved by experience — you cannot imagine how much she has improved since last you saw her."

"I am extremely sorry, if my visit has been the cause of bringing to your painful recollection a thing of which I could wish, with very great respect, that you, madam, or Belinda either, might never again think. She shall not, however, suffer any inconvenience by my being in the house. I shall never forget the kindly and familiar manner in which I have been treated by you. I wish you all well, not excepting —; good bye."

Rowland left the house with tears in his eyes, which, Esq. Howard perceiving, walked by the side of his horse two or three miles, with an expectation that he should yet be able to convince him of his daughter's honorable motives at the time of the disruption, and consistent conduct since, but without success.

Another solitary year rolled round, and Belinda was sitting at her chamber window, musing upon the neglect in which she was passing her days, the vanity of the events of former times, and her prospects for the future, when the carriage of Fitz Rowland drove rapidly by. She was filled with apprehensions. White veils were floating in the wind, and glad, gleeful faces were turned towards the house. The sight of a funeral procession, of pall and shroud, and tears, and wringing hands would have been a thousand times less painful. The same day, at dinner, she asked her father if he saw Rowland's carriage pass? He answered that he had not, and thought she must have mistaken some other for his, as the great road ran at a considerable distance from the house. A jealous eye is quick in perception, and cannot easily mistake. The suspicions of Belinda were soon confirmed by a vociferous youngster's coming in, and asking her if she was acquainted with Fitz Rowland, from the Thames, and saying that he had just passed on his way home with his newly married wife. Belinda turned ghastly pale, exclaimed, "my last hope has now vanished," retired to her room, and threw herself across her bed, and wept as Rowland once had done.****

When Dionisious, the cruel Sicilian tyrant, was deposed from a throne which his father had reared by artifice and stratagem; held by acts of the most incredible barbarity; and transmitted to his son, stained with the blood of his peaceable subjects, he had become so habituated to commanding, and so fond of being obeyed, that he thought it impossible to live without them.

That his disposition might be in some degree gratified, by giving law and inflicting punishment, he established a small school, which, with a haughty brow, himself supervised. In the same manner, Belinda, when she was precipitated from the pinnacle of fame, upon which, in imagination, she had been standing, and when her power of absolute rule over the hearts and affections of men was lost, determined to make herself conspicuous in a way scarcely less reprehensible than she had formerly. She had become extremely fond of attending theatres, masquerades, and balls of every description, but she gave all these up, as bringing herself too much on a level with the rest of her race, and pretending to new and large accessions of grace, appointed public meetings for religious improvement. She would always address the assembly herself, and often, what she said, would, in its proper place, have been unexceptionable. In her harangues she would boast and bluster with all the flourish of female oratory. In her petitions there always was a lengthy preamble, full of the most frightful denouncements, and at the close, a prayer for every body but herself. She was assisted and encouraged in these acts of arrant folly, by Mrs. Pomeroy, an old lady of perhaps better intentions, but far past her prime — in mind as well as in body. She could, however, speak with considerable fluency, if not with logical reasoning; and her wild, wandering speculations, and extravagant gesticulation were thought sometimes to have a beneficial effect.

This old lady (let us all unite in blessing her!) soon spread the fame of Belinda over the whole country, as a perfect pattern by which others might very much improve themselves in practising the christian virtues. To listen to her advice — to agree with her in sentiment, or to favor the opinion that it was not contrary to any thing in the bible or in nature for women to expose themselves to the public gaze and deliver extempore speeches, on subjects of vital importance, was sufficient to give one a name among the *living*. But three woes to him who differed with our heroine in the most trivial matter; he was bruited to the world as a disbeliever in all that is high and holy — as impious almost beyond the possibility of recovery. She was represented as being capable of speaking upon doubtful questions in divinity; and as being the most fit and proper person to whom one, in a state of indecision, could go for advice. This was, I say, the opinion of Belinda's coadjutor in the grand scheme of evangelizing the world, and she no doubt thought herself right. We all think ourselves correct in our religious *opinions*. This is a self-evident proposition. Every man living has a thousand times found himself mistaken in his notion of things, and yet he has never been able to carry his wisdom or his reason so far as to believe that what he thought was right or wrong, was not so, even though all the world might differ with him. This is not only true of those who establish every thing by tracing the effect back to the cause, before giving it a place among their settled notions, but also of those whose whims or caprices deserve not to be dignified with the name of thought.

I have been very delicate in speaking of the spiritual teachings of Belinda, through the fear that it might be thought I was willing to cast a slur upon religion, or turn it to ridicule. Nothing could be farther from my intention or feelings upon the subject. No where, in my opinion, does it appear to so great an advantage as when, in reality, it affects the female character, and is made its peculiar ornament. And yet, I shall presume to say, once for all, that when it plays round the head, but comes not near the heart — when it dwells upon the tongue, but allays not the dispositions, it does not have so desirable a tendency.

CHAPTER VII.

Were I writing a mere novel, or were I composing merely to pass time away, or for the pleasure of the moment, by putting upon paper whatever strange or curious thing might present itself to my mind, then my plan should be very different from the course which I have adopted. It would never have entered my head to close a piece of fiction in the manner this is to end; but since I have undertaken to set down a few of the most important and interesting events in the life of Belinda, as a lesson for mankind, (begging their pardon,) and a sort of beacon to point out (save the mark!) some dangerous shoals to the sex. I cannot, though I feel myself unequal to the task, pass over the closing scene without making an attempt at description. I promise if ever I write again, to choose a more agreeable subject. — It is, however, no small satisfaction to a reader, and atones — when we can keep clear of critics — for considerable faults, when he knows the piece which he is perusing to be true — when he knows that however unpleasant any particular incident may be, it actually occurred; and that the characters were really beings of his own species, — not that the good were angels, and the bad, devils. It detracts very much from our entertainment, and considerably lessens the impression which a tale is calculated to make upon our minds, when we reflect that, perhaps such persons as the actors are represented to be, never were born; and that the scenes presented to our view, have no existence in real life. I hope such considerations as these may not rob what I have written, or have yet to write, of the little interest which my strict regard for truth allows me to give it. I shall be ambitious only to paint the picture true to the original, without vainly endeavoring to improve upon nature.

Belinda, was now in the height of her vogue as a saint. Like Joan of Arc, she was looked upon as a prodigy. Even those who felt opposed, as a general practice, to females leaving that retirement in which they appear to so great an advantage, and where they are able to confer a real blessing upon them who seek it in its proper place, hesitated about condemning too hastily so great a semblance of sanctity, and thought Miss Howard and Mrs. Pomeroy should be considered as exceptions to the rule, or as something wonderful, something out of the regular order of things, such as we have a right to expect once in an age. But great numbers, of all ranks in society, thought it the extreme of folly and impiety to question the sincerity of their zeal; they thought a thing so obvious ought to be taken for granted; exempted entirely from investigation; and that a certain foolish and barbarous usage recommended by the man called Paul, who, it was said, never liked the ladies very well himself, was now become quite obsolete, and should be forever exploded. I do not know that either Belinda or her aid-de-camp, the old lady of whom I spoke before, ever dispossessed an unclean spirit with a word, at least in obstinate cases, but they were said to have done the same thing by their ghostly advice, and prevailing intercession, and of this, therefore, I would not wish to be understood as having spoken. But having, myself, seen them placed upon an elevated stand, without the least appearance of modest reserve, and in an important tone, deliver set speeches to five hundred persons at once, making the vulgar stare and laugh, and decent men ashamed — and believing that the better part, even of the "better half" of mankind, together with that book, which Protestants call "the only rule of faith and *practice*," is on my side, I thought I should be safe in saying what has been said upon this very delicate subject.

Eight years had now elapsed since McLeod so gallantly fought his way from the house of Esquire Howard, and the celebrity of Belinda as a counsellor, gave her an opportunity of again enjoying the public and private company of every class, age, and sex. She was no pettifogger, but, like a lawyer, perfect in his profession, was prepared at any time to give correct advice, either by word of mouth or by writing — accepting, of course, the usual fees. Among the many who were indebted to her good offices for inward peace, I shall only particularize one, and what I say of him shall be taken from the confessions of his own mouth. Bickerstaff, sometimes called the shepherd, I suppose from the occupation of his forefathers, lived in ease and affluence, about two miles from the Clifton Hall. His age, at the time of which I speak, was about thirty years. His wife was one of those women "whose price," Solomon says, "is far above rubies — the heart of her husband might have safely trusted in her, so that he should have had no need of spoil, and she will do him good and not evil all the days of her life." Prov. xxxi. 10, 11, 12. Bickerstaff was extensively engaged in the mercantile business, and a very fit person to stand behind a counter, than which I am not prepared to pass any greater encomium upon his character. He seldom looked an honest man in the face, but, like some animals of the canine species, seemed to shun the eye of superior beings. Impudence, unquestionably, is no proof of innocence; still, I see no sufficient reason why a man of integrity, and a clear conscience, may not fold his arms with unconcern, and stand the stare of the whole world, without blushing. From my very limited observations upon human nature, I have been led to conclude that the blush is a kind of spirit. I also believe in the transmigration of such spirits as this. I believe that a lady may be so unfortunate as to be deprived of this soul of beauty and virtue before she dies, so that she shall not be able, were it to save her life, to make this heavenly rainbow, this interpreter of the heart, adorn her cheek, without the help of rouge. And he into whose body this subtle spirit has transmigrated, cannot prevent it from flushing his countenance whenever he appears in company, and playing about his eyes like the fantastical ignis fatuus. When it is seen at the post where the wise hand of heaven ordained it to stand sentry, it is a sign of virtue; when it leaves that and occupies another, it becomes the signal of guilt.

Bickerstaff, pretending great concern about his future destiny, and being able to get no relief from what the parson or his bible told him, went to Belinda and asked her, with tears in his eyes, what he must do to escape impending ruin. She soon informed him that the way was so plain that though he were a fool — which she was by no means prepared to admit — there could not be the least danger of his erring therein. "You have a chart," says she, "an infallible chart, in which you will find a correct description of the track to be pursued. The rocks and shoals are distinctly marked. We are not required to believe all that even good men have spoken and written since the christian era commenced. Not all their tenets are binding upon us, but those only which we find in this book; though they may have marked them as essential. Freedom of conscience I consider not only as a very great desideratum, but as really indispensable to the christian character. If you are compelled to believe a thing in which you ought to have faith, who is the better for your forced assent? — Let us, then, be governed by nothing but our bible and our reason. We find nothing there about *Christ's viceregent upon earth*, or his half-way house. I do not know as Calvin's frightful decrees have a record in a very conspicuous place. I have not yet discovered any thing positive about Dr. Pusey's long chain of bishops with their coat-tails and surplice sleeves pinned together. Miller's new-fangled notions are singularly obscure. I do not say that all or any of those systems are false; but they are not plain. The *way-faring man* understands them not. None but doctors in divinity can comprehend their meaning and application; they, therefore, are not essential, however curious. We are commanded to believe — to love — and to serve, as the conditions upon which peace and safety are to be granted."

"Are we not," says Bickerstaff in a whisper, "commanded to love one another, too, Belinda? I have gone this far, for I love you as myself."

"This positive mandate, in certain cases, is very easily obeyed, and in others with the greatest difficulty. So far as you, Bickerstaff, are concerned, without hesitancy I can say, too, and that from my heart, I love you as myself."

"The satisfaction which that expression yields me, is only surpassed by the happiness I feel on account of the encouraging hopes which your religious instruction has planted within my breast. Like Bunyan's pilgrim, I was oppressed with a burden too heavy for any man to bear. But you have cut the cords which bound it to my back, and brought me quick relief. I feel that I ought to exercise a degree of gratitude and love towards you, Belinda, next to that which I owe to our blessed Lord. He is my Savior, and you are the instrument of my salvation. Both the one and the other I love with all my heart."

"I am very happy, my dear Bickerstaff, to hear you express your confidence that you 'have passed from death unto life,' and in seeing its sure effects — love and gratitude. Nothing is more imperative upon us than love of our fellow creatures, and, as it is enjoined, I confess I love you freely."

"My dear Belinda, I am almost compelled to use the language which, under similar circumstances, escaped the lips of our greatest naval hero, Lord Nelson. Addressing himself to Lady Hamilton, (whom he loved as I do you,) and speaking of his wife, (whom he disliked as I do Josephine,) he says — 'I hope we shall enjoy many happy years together, when that *impediment* shall be removed, if God please, and be surrounded by our children's children."

"We need not wait for that event to enjoy the *knowledge* of each other's love. There is a secret, undefinable pleasure in knowing that we occupy a place in another's heart."

If there had been any thing like a principle of honor in one, or of virtue in the other — to say nothing of the spirit of that religion which they professed — I would not be obliged to break off the dialogue between the goddess and him who worshipped at her shrine, so abruptly. But I dare not follow them another step, through the fear of spoiling my book. The transmigration of the goblin blush, however, took place, and, like some churchyard spectre, it still wildly wanders about the sheepish face of the indecorous and uncurbable Bickerstaff.

The shepherd's wife was not naturally of a jealous disposition, nor did her tongue, intended for nobler uses, delight in loathsome ribaldry; still she, no doubt, felt indignant, and could not entirely suppress her feelings, when she reflected that one who had filched from her a thing which she so highly prized, her husband's love, should be exalted to the skies as something superior to the generality of mortals. This excellent, but injured, lady privately conjured Bickerstaff, by all that was lovely, by all that was reputable, by all that was sacred, to desist, and save her swelling heart from bursting! She offered yet to forgive him — she could not cease to love him if she would. This was said in a whisper, in her chamber, but it appeared as if the birds of the air told it, and spread the news abroad. In return she received insult and abuse, which she bore in a manner which ought to atone for all the fault of all her sex. Such characters, in a tale like this, may be compared to the green spots in the great desert of Africa. They form resting places where the mind recruits, gains confidence, and passes on with pleasure. I, too, am particularly happy in coming across, now and then, one for another reason, and that is to save myself from the imputation of misanthropy. The conduct of this lady was worthy of all praise, yet she was not only hooted at by the deceived multitude, but neglected and exposed by the man who had sworn to cherish and protect her. Bickerstaff's visits, under the mask of religion, were continued at the house of Esq. Howard, while the expostulating smile which met him at his own door, was disdainfully frowned back whence it came, to expire in silent sighs. Who would not wish to share in the meritorious act of purchasing a rope to suspend the rascal high in air? If there is any thing that would excite my mirth and jollity, 'twould be to see a wretch like this dangling at a gallows — a lofty gallows, and substantial, like that on which the wicked Hamon hanged, and which, like him, he had so well deserved.

Things were at this pass when Theodore Unwin, a young gentleman of a cultivated mind and polished manners, first appeared in the neighborhood of the Clifton Hall. His business was to choose, at his own discretion, and obtain an eligible situation in that part of the country for his father, C. Unwin, Esq., and family, who were to follow as soon as they received advice that the necessary preparations were made for their comfortable reception. He had long been considered, by all who knew him, as uncommonly discreet, and apt to premeditate, so that he seldom had cause to repent having undertaken any scheme or project whatever. And, indeed, I will submit it to better judges than myself, whether his having arrived at the mature age of twenty-seven, without being once involved in the happy misery of love, or having tried the pleasing, dreadful realities of marriage was not a sufficient proof of this. But

Solon refused to pronounce the rich King Croesus wise and happy, because he was not yet dead; and I am not prepared to dispute with so great a man.

Strange as it may sound, it is no more strange than true, the very first time the sapient Theodore saw Belinda, even before he saw her face, from her form and gesture, his impression was a strong predilection in her favor. He looked upon her like Adam, when he first saw Eve, and felt that he had lost a rib, that there was something wanting to make him complete in himself, and that there now was an opportunity offered of supplying the deficiency. He made some inquiries about her name, residence, and character, with the poor chance a stranger has of learning any thing correctly of the latter, and was satisfied that she was the very person, for whom a thousand happy accidents and chances had kept him. For, notwithstanding all that has been said, the character of Belinda was, at this time, in certain quarters, held in high estimation. She was the oracle of the day — in all her ways oraculous.

Perhaps the sight of Belinda had some influence with Theodore, in inducing him to make choice of a situation about a mile from the Clifton Hall. However this might be, he thought the beauty of the prospect, the salubrity of the climate, and the kindly disposition of the people, surpassed those of any other part of North America. — He accordingly made his purchases, and resolved to make the shores of Lake Erie his home for the rest of his life. His heart beat more quickly than it ever had before; his mind was excited with hope; his spirits were in an unusual flutter, and, like a man under the influence of that dire demon, the spirit of rum, he was entirely incapable of sober judgment, and yet was full of confidence in the infallibility of his conclusions.

Thus blindfolded, Theodore, the first Sunday after his coming into the place, attended church, where the luminous occidental star shone forth with peculiar radiance, and so attracted his attention, and so eclipsed every surrounding object with its insupportable blaze, as entirely to captivate him, and make him forget that he was in a temple not devoted to the worship of a visible and material god. I am afraid that the words of the messenger of the Great King, that day, sounded to Theodore like idle tales, which he neither believed nor disbelieved.

Belinda had not been unobservant, and quickly perceived that she had not yet lost her power to charm. When the service was ended, and the congregation dismissed — the crowd being very dense before the church door — she was apparently elbowed out of her intended path, and full of surprise found herself at the side of Theodore.

"Would it be unpardonable, fair lady," said Theodore, "in a stranger, to offer his assistance at such a time and in such a place as this? Please take my arm."

"I ought rather to beg *your* pardon, kind sir," replied Belinda, "for intruding thus upon you. I pray you will not think me so unacquainted [taking his arm] with prudentials, as to have purposely found my way to a place which, after all, is not unpleasant. I never witnessed, in my life, such rude behavior from the people of this parish. They rushed from the house as if it had been a prison, and the minister had been sent to open wide the doors, instead of to deliver them from an incarceration of a different and more dreadful nature."

"It, however, speaks well for the neighborhood, to see so great a number at a place of public worship."

"Yes, but it is to be feared that they were induced to come hither by many different motives. Were we to deduct from this mixed mass of sheep and goats those who came *to see and to be seen* — if my heart misgives me not — those whose object was *to hear*, would make a small remainder."

"Well, certainly," replied Theodore, "that is too little thought of. Indeed, I should almost shrink from close examination to-day myself, for fear of being classed among the goats by you, lady."

"O, my dear sir, you must not think my charity so meagre; for although I am not often hasty in conclusions, yet, when *first* I saw your thoughtful brow, my impression was ———. Pardon me, it is not always right to *speak* our thoughts."

"Allow me, ere we part, to inquire what might be your father's name, and where his and your happy home?"

"His name is Howard, and we are at the gate of what you please to call a happy home. And now, I will take no excuse, you shall walk in and share its comforts."

"I accept, Miss Howard, your very agreeable invitation, with many hearty thanks."

Theodore was now beyond his depth—he was within the current, and rapidly approaching a tremendous vortex. He thought his prospects for the future more promising than they had ever before been, while the fact was plainly the very contrary — they had never been half so perilous. He spent the afternoon with Belinda; was pleased with the favorable disposition of her parents, as well as lost in admiration of the first example he had ever found, where there existed perfect harmony between mind and matter, or where there was extrinsic beauty in perfection, combined with intrinsic piety and amiability in the same degree; and returned to his lodgings exulting in his wonderful success. "Happy man!" said Theodore to himself, as he passed the gate, (having heard a few of Belinda's kind compliments, perceived the throbbings of her heart in its earliest love, and even felt the electrifying touch of her lips,) "happy man," said he, "I am the happiest man alive." From this time the intervals between the visits of Theodore at the Clifton Hall were very short, until the arrival of his father, and the rest of the family, about six months after his acquaintance with Belinda. This nettled the shepherd very much. He was chafed terribly by the conduct of Theodore, but as some faint idea of the *name* of honor remained, in some occult corner of his breast or brain, he hesitated about coming out in open opposition, and claiming his rightful property. There soon was a close intimacy between the families of Esqrs. Howard and Unwin, and particularly between Miss Juliet Unwin and Belinda, but time showed that there was no chemical affinity — and what is friendship, so called, without it? Juliet declared her convictions to be that Belinda was a pious and excellent girl, and that her brother, by marrying her, would not only get to himself a wife whose love would stand the test of sickness and old age, but form a connection which would give them a respectable stand in the neighborhood.

Every thing appeared to conspire to favor Belinda's intentions of terminating her career as a general lover. She seriously and deliberately resolved to put an end to the fluctuations of unmeaning courtship, by giving her hand to Theodore forever. Bickerstaff had continued his visits, under various pretensions, until Belinda saw that the vigilance of the acute Unwins rendered it unsafe any longer to admit him. One evening, in the presence of Theodore and her father's family, he was accordingly informed that it would not be convenient for her to receive his company again for some time, as she would be otherwise engaged. With great emotion, he replied that he looked upon her as his spiritual mother, and feared he should go back again and become as bad as ever he was, if she did not still nurture him with her wholesome advice. Belinda said, that if he had received any assistance from her poor words, she was extremely happy, but did not wish to ascribe it to herself. She, however, had nothing more — nothing new to tell him, and he must endeavor to improve upon the means within his reach. She did not wish him to ask her any more questions, nor for the future to frequent her father's house on her account. Bickerstaff bid her adieu, and with evident chagrin, grumbling and mumbling, found his way through a stormy and dark night to his own house, where good advice, had he wanted it, was cheap and genuine. He railed against the whole sex indiscriminately — their instability, falsity, and worthlessness, without thinking that if he should go no farther than his own house, the balance would be in their favor. It has been often said by man, that woman is like Luna, subject to many phases; but himself, like Phoebus, regular and unchangeable. I shall not even give an opinion as to the justness of this observation. Those who speak in terms of general condemnation of whole divisions, states, or denominations of people, are very apt to render themselves suspected. Those who speak so positively in praise of their own sex or sect, might, perhaps, be better employed in making themselves an example of what they aver to be true. "Let him who is without sin cast a stone at her."

Mr. and Mrs. Howard, supposing Brock to be dead, having never once heard from him during nine long and anxious years, had ceased to mourn, and were pleased with the prospect of seeing the blank which that event had made in their family, filled up by the adoption of Theodore. They also felt as if they were about to be relieved from a still greater load than the grief of tender parents for the loss of a dutiful son — that of a painful solicitude for the fate of Belinda. This, like some pulmonary disease, was insensibly consuming the vital parts, and rendering uncertain life a burden. Theodore had asked and obtained the free consent, both of his own parents and those of Belinda, to a union with her, who held, with steady grasp, the reins by which he was controlled.

About this time, Brock, to the unspeakable happiness of his friends, returned home. His parents received him as from the grave, and his sister hoped her character now to be so well *established* as, instead of causing him to retire into voluntary banishment, to be the greatest inducement to him to spend his days with those of kindred blood. It seems that he had made the city of Detroit, Michigan, his principal place of residence while numbered among the dead. He kept a retail store for several years on —————— street, Detroit; and yet, though the name of the *Canadian coquette* was familiar to many in the place, he was never known to be her brother. He had held a regular correspondence, during the whole time of his absence, with some confidential friend in the vicinity, and being advised that Belinda had quite retrieved her good name, and was likely to be soon united by those two strong links, love and law, with a gentleman of undoubted worth, had resolved to witness the consummation of a thing which was to prove him a false prophet. One day, soon after Brock's return, Bickerstaff, notwithstanding what had passed between him and Belinda, called at the Clifton Hall. Esq. Howard, however, knowing that he was looked upon by many as a suspicious character, whether he did so himself or not, immediately gave him to understand by a hint in the coarsest and roughest style, that he was not welcome at his house.

The shepherd could no longer control his rage, but determined, even at the expense of his own reputation, to revenge the insult which he had received from an arrogant father of a fickle beauty. — Fearing that his resolution would fail him, and ingratitude, treason, and revolt consequently escape due punishment, he went directly to Esq. Unwin's. Professing the most disinterested zeal for happiness of his friend Theodore, he enquired whether the report of his intended marriage with Miss Howard were founded in truth. Unwin frankly confessed his intention of making her his wife, and asked the shepherd if he thought her not a worthy person? The question was answered by a shrug of the shoulders and a lowering of the brow.

"I do believe you are my friend, Bickerstaff," said Theodore, the color of his face changing, "but why can you not speak your thoughts? Those contortions of the body always mean something, and that is more than can be said of words themselves; but as their signification is uncertain, a confidential friend should never use them. Tell me what you know of her."

"Our acquaintance has been very short, and it would be presuming upon your confidence — it would be supposing you to think as much of me as I do of you, if I should tell you all I know of one you love *too well*."

"Too well! that is impossible. But torture me no longer; tell me what you know, and prove it, too. Be careful that you assert nothing which you are not prepared to substantiate."

"She, upon whom you doat, is very fair of face."

"And all within is perfect harmony — her dispositions amiable — her intellectual powers strong."

"If that be correct — and I have not yet disputed it — then you possess a greater knowledge of the lady than myself."

"You certainly have no intention of disputing it?"

"No: I have many things to say, but *you* are not prepared to hear them now. Truth is a serious thing!"

"*Some* truths are serious; — 'twould be a serious thing to see the world on fire, and this, Bickerstaff, shall be seen before Belinda prove unworthy of my love."

"Then doomsday must be rapidly approaching, and you would do well to think of something more befitting that eventful period, than that of wiving with a ——, with Miss Howard."

"With a what? It is well you did suppress a word, and call her by her proper name, for my hand was clenched, and rising of itself, to fall upon your head, when, fortunately, you paused, and saved your life — and mine."

"You spit against the wind, Theodore, when you refuse to hear what would be for your own advantage, and must expect some sprinklings of your venom to fall back."

"I beg your pardon sir, and confess I was too quickly moved. My temper, perhaps, is naturally too warm, too easily excited, but I will now endeavor to keep cool, and hear you through."

"Guard well your passions, exercise your reason, and cease to love but for a moment, while I speak, that you may understand. I *fear* — nay, I *know* Belinda is not uncontaminated; and would you wish to call that yours which is another's?"

"Ha! Beelzebub, thou chief of devils, how came you to slip your chain, and in the shape of a monstrous toad, find your way to my ear, swelling with foul lies. Now if I had Ithuriel's spear, to touch you with its point, I might see the true shape of one of those spirits accursed, which 'dared the Omnipotent to arms.'"

"I can prove all that I have said, by indubitable testimony, but hope you will not push the thing to that extreme."

"Bring on your witnesses, in rank and file, stronger than Xerxes' army, and make them all swear by the whole Pantheon, but expect me not to believe them. I am not quite so credulous as Othello — Belinda is a thousand times more innocent than Desdemona, and you are a less excusable defamer than Iago, and more profound in villanies. But I *will push the thing to the extreme* of demonstration, and drag the wretch at whose existence you have hinted, into daylight, or make you suffer in his place. I am no lawyer, but from the fame of the constitution of this great empire, from the fact that it is admired by all wise men, and styled the *perfection of reason* all over the world, I infer that there will be something found in the complete system of English jurisprudence, which will loose the arm of justice — throttle such bloodsuckers of society as yourself, and give security to helpless innocence. I'll call you Iago, and your *fabled* miscreant, (for I am sure he has no being,) we will denominate Cassio; now, sir, point him out, or prepare to defend yourself."

"Cassio was an honorable man, and Desdemona was as pure as the untrodden snow, she therefore does not fairly represent the false Belinda!"

"False! 'Tis by an effort I restrain my ire; but proceed with your vile calumnies — with your midnight-concocted tale, wherein you have, 'tis plain, been by the black powers assisted. I promise, say what you will, to give you safe conduct from the house."

"I must confess the truth to my shame. I am the man, for whose innocence you so strenuously plead, but not alone in guilt. Here is a paper, which will set all to rights, and save you from otherwise inevitable ruin. Here McLeod, one of her first lovers, certifies that he and Belinda were as intimate as Anthony and Cleopatra, some eight or ten years since. I took the pains to procure this certificate, partly to convince you, my young friend, of your dangerous delusion, and partly to save myself from damage in case of a prosecution, with which the father of this commoner has threatened me. I have *robbed* no man of his right — what I have, or have had, has been procured by fair *purchase*, and if there was a sin in that, I have repented of the crime, and hope to be forgiven. Let us draw the bonds of friendship still closer than ever between us. I give the thoughts of the unkind words which you have used, all to oblivion. Your blood was then in a state of ebullition, and your language was the escaping effervescence — the evaporation of ephemeral love."

"Ephemeral love belongs to brutes like you — mine and Belinda's like that of the spirits of light, will be eternal. That you are guilty, and McLeod too, whoever he may be, I have no reason to doubt, but not of what you make your boast. I wonder that infinite mercy and forbearance can restrain the thunderbolts of justice for a moment. But think not that heaven is accessary to your deeds. The time will come when your compunctions will be something keener than a careless *'hope to be forgiven!'* I tell thee to thy teeth, thou liest, execrable wretch. What! two perfidious men conspire to blast the hopes, by darkening with blackest shades, the character of one whose body, soul and name, are all alike immaculate? I will not so much as inquire of a single person, whether what you have said be true or not. I know it to be false. Avaunt! thou compound of all that is base and bad."

Bickerstaff had not a moment to lose; the least hesitation might have proved fatal — a word might have cost him his life, and he prudently thought the shortest way to the street the safest.

CHAPTER VIII.

The same afternoon of the conference, or rather the quarrel between Theodore and his quondam friend, Juliet, the particular friend of Belinda, had been at the house of Bickerstaff, and returned just as he went out from her father's. She had been informed by that broken hearted lady, the shepherd's wife, of the true state of affairs, without extenuation or exaggeration, and her unpretending manner forced conviction upon the mind of Juliet.

The changes which now ensued, show that there is a difference between friendship and love, let the disbelievers in Hymen's divinity say what they will. Theodore had made known to his parents the business of Bickerstaff at the house, and how he had attempted to persuade him to turn his back upon the only one he ever loved, and disbelieve a thing, the truth of which, he had ocularly demonstrated, and no other kind of demonstration asked he for, in such a case. Having seen Belinda, was sufficient proof of her innocence. Juliet was prepared to substantiate all that Bickerstaff had said, believing it to be true. This astonished and offended her brother, but his mind was not to be changed. Her father withdrew his consent to the conjugation, and declared that if it did take place, it would be without his or Mrs. Unwin's approval. The house was in an uproar. Theodore thought the whole family insane, and determined to see the fair and faultless, but defamed Belinda, that very evening, and let her know, that although *the people might imagine a vain thing*, his affections would remain forever quiescent. His mother expostulated with him, advised him not to be too hasty, said that if Miss Howard was innocent, there could be no great harm in a short delay, and that genuine virtue would ultimately command respect. But it were easier to "draw out Leviathan with a hook," or tie up the whirlwind with a silken thread, than to govern a lover, a mad lover, by the force of reason and argumentation. It was now night, a clear and frosty night in the middle of a Canadian winter. Theodore ordered his horse and sleigh. Juliet concealed his coat and boots, and refused to discover them, though both persuasions and menaces were multiplied. A vain effort at discomfiture! There was a fire burning within the breast of Theodore which enabled him very comfortably to dispense with any extra wool of bleating sheep, or hide of lowing kine. He left the house heavily, slamming the door behind him, and was on his way towards the magnet by which he was irresistibly attracted. A southerner, who has never traveled, can have no idea of our hibernal roads, solid as marble, and transparent as glass, over the surface of lakes and rivers — reflecting back the stare with almost equal radiance — and bellowing like a thing of real life. One would be apt to think old Neptune bound beneath, and laboring to extricate himself.

Theodore drove like Mahommed when on his way to Mecca; his horse struck fire with his feet at every step; and a minute scarce elapsed between his father's and his destination.

Belinda received him with a smile, which cheered his heart and more than balanced all that her detractors could invent. The shepherd's gratuitous and most malicious tale was soon adverted to, and as soon satisfactorily disproved by artful conduct. Miss Howard was struck with horror at the very words — surprised that she, who had never loved before in all her life, — who had always been remarkable for her modest, decent reserve, and natural antipathy to the company of men in general, should possibly become the subject of reports so foul; and hoped if all the world beside allowed themselves to be imposed upon, yet Theodore would never deviate from truth and holy love.

"If an angel from heaven," said Theodore, "should tell me any thing to your prejudice, I would not believe it. And now, it is useless to protract, without utility, our present state of suspense, and give that unruly member, the tongue, which has been set on fire by a torch lit at the flames of bottomless perdition, time to work its deep designs. Insidious means are being used to blast our fair prospects. A train has been artfully laid. A slow match has been applied, to explode our mutual love and sever the strong links which attach our hearts."

"A great explosion cannot happen," replies Belinda, "while the cavities of our soul (I use the word in the singular, considering what once were two, now commixed and one) are free from combustible matter; — or while love, innocence, and religion occupy our whole mind and every avenue which leads to it. I am not afraid to stand the test of revealing time and let the tongue of the shepherds, or goatherds either, have liberty to do its worst, — for Mr. Addison says that 'a lampoon or a satire does not carry in it robbery or murder;' — but I could not deny you, my dear Theodore, any thing which you might ask, even if it were to become your wife to-morrow. Indeed, I feel as if the citadel of my heart had been taken by storm and placed at the discretion of a foreign governor. That governor, I am pleased to think, is yourself, Theodore, and I shall, consequently, be very happy to agree to any terms you may propound, as to the time and manner of your taking possession of the whole."

When Belinda's glib tongue stood still, Unwin detected himself staring at her with a fixed gaze, like a charmed serpent at an Indian musician.

"My dear, how happy shall I be," he exclaimed, "when I can spend whole days, and weeks, and months in the unalloyed pleasure of your company! And since you have left the commencement of that felicitous epoch to my own appointment, I will say — compelled by circumstances — three long weeks from to-day, which will be the twenty-second of February, 1843. Approve of this, my own Belinda, and liars on earth will in vain combine with their father below to change my resolution."

"I do believe," returns Miss Howard, "that our minds and affections are literally one. Your words are precisely those I would have used — the time the same I would have specified, had it been left to me."

With love poured forth in terms not understood by every one conversant with the English language, Theodore took his leave — seated himself again behind the fractious *Alborak*, and found himself at home — went to bed to continue, in visions of the night, his waking dreams.

Bickerstaff made no scruple in repeating what he had told Theodore, or in showing Mack's certificate, — for which he had probably paid a clever sum of money, — wherever there appeared the faintest prospect of its promoting his interests. The report soon reached the ears of Brock, who hooted his informant from his presence as a vile traducer, second only in perfidy to the first inventor of the falsehood. He felt, however, as did his parents, that there was too much reason for believing all, and more than had been brought to light. But it is an effort too great for the human mind, when the general good seems to require us to love our neighbor *better* than ourselves. It is sufficient that we love him as ourself, and no more than this is requisite, I apprehend, to make the proper scale preponderate. Upon this principle let the world pardon the Howards for not disclosing what they *knew*, and thereby injuring themselves for others' benefit. Nothing was neglected by Belinda's friends to prevent Theodore from looking about him, by keeping up the excitement of his mind; and to disabuse the public in regard to her, by counter suppositions and transmutations.

Theodore had a superstitious reverence for the will of his father and mother. This came near saving him. He told them he would never marry without their liberty; but if permission were not given in the present case — if he were not allowed to unite with one to whom he was bound by many solemn oaths — one whom he loved, and by whom he was affectionately regarded, they should never see his face again; but that he would find a distant home, and spend his few remaining wretched days in picking roots and berries for a sustenance, upon the most southern cape of Van Dieman's land.

"By granting my request," said he, in a tone of most submissive but earnest supplication, "you will confer a great blessing — render me happy through life — and lay me under an additional debt of gratitude, which I know can never be fully canceled. But while the principal remains unpaid, Belinda and myself, when you are old, will endeavor to discharge, by anticipating all your wants, the accumulating interest at high percentage. On the other hand, by allowing your minds to be biased against the most worthy, as well as the fairest and most lovely of woman kind, by the vague and unqualified assertions of a man whose groveling sentiments and bestial propensities fit him only to rove the desert with the tiger and the bear — and, by consequently denying my humble petition, joining my enemy against me, and assisting in publicly branding, with the last degree of ignominy, an innocent girl — by doing this, I say, positively, you will procure either my death, or my banishment to a penal isle remote. — As sure as there are powers above or powers below, I will be buried, banished, or married, in less than twenty days!"

The question now assumed a more serious aspect.

Mrs. Unwin advised, as opposition appeared useless, that they should agree, with seeming satisfaction and without a moment's delay, to Theodore's wishes. It might be for the best, and he might, after all, before the day arrived, see something which would change his fixed determination.

Her husband, however, was made of sterner stuff. He said that he now felt himself in the situation of the great Mithridates, king of Pontus, who, when his dominions were invaded by the greedy Romans, and his family like to be made prisoners and dragged through the streets of the imperial city to grace the proud victor's triumph, sent a swift messenger to offer the ladies of his court their choice of death, in three different ways — the bowl, the rope, or the sword. So I shall say to Theodore. Let him take which he thinks most advantageous of the three he has named — it is death to make the best of it. I'll not oppose him any farther."

This reply was immediately communicated to Theodore by his mother, who, of course, softened its crustiness considerably with a maternal accent. Though merely toleration of a thing highly disapproved of, this quite satisfied his fastidious mind, and removed all apprehensions of disappointment in pursuit or dissatisfaction in enjoyment. As soon as Juliet was acquainted with the progress her brother had made — how, by intimidation, he had gained upon his parents; — when she knew that the wedding day was appointed, and that the manor-house (Esq. Unwin's) was to be divided, and Belinda soon to become mistress of one half of it, she decided upon leaving home and remaining absent until either the public or her brother was lastingly unfooled. Theodore entreated her not to expose herself to shame and penury by her violent and indecent opposition to a match which did not so immediately affect her. But her phrenological developments very plainly showed that she had a mind of her own. Indeed, though she was in other respects amiably disposed, her untractableness amounted almost to obstinacy. She was as great a paradox as her brother — tender-hearted as a child — unpersuadable as a freebooter!

They parted, weeping for each other, and yet — each inflexibly fixed in pre-established opinions — never once thought of a compromise. Juliet, the next morning, left for Chatham, a beautiful and rapidly increasing town, situated upon the two banks of the Thames, and at nearly equal distances from the three lakes Erie, St. Clair, and Huron. This town, having every advantage from its location, in the centre of the most fertile district in the Province; and, from the nature of the country, being more easy of access than any other part or point whatever, with an enterprising population, is plainly destined to become, at no distant period, a place of immense business and importance.

By a singular accident, Juliet here fell in with Mrs. Pomeroy, the good old preacher-lady, notable in the history of Miss Howard. It would be no more than justice to observe here, that this *true veteran* had withdrawn from her connexion with our heroine, and, though happily unsuccessful in her attempt to raise a corps of Amazonian warriors, shrunk not from bearing the brunt alone, but steadily pursued her purpose of subjugating the world to the sway of the benign sceptre. Her persevering industry excites my admiration and forbids my withholding from her the well earned appelation of *"the great apostle of the fair."* It is a question, however, whether, if *the great apostle of the Gentiles* were now living, there would be room for them both upon this little ball. A moment's thought before we decide, or perhaps, we had better not decide at all. Let the world wag. Juliet took rooms with the old lady, and, as she pleased to express herself, awaited with impatience the news of some dreadful concussion among the highlands.

I had almost forgotten the lovely Belinda, but shall now go back to the Clifton Hall, give her a friendly shake by the hand, and endeavor, before the wedding day arrives, to make up friends. The kindly disposition which she always manifested towards her brothers and sisters; the respectful attention which she paid to her parents; and the general propriety of her whole visible deportment, entitle her to no small share of esteem.

Some ten days previous to that which was to terminate all strife, even Belinda — though for so many years accustomed to wonderful things — was astonished and shocked by the perusal of the underwritten billet, received through the postoffice. It was dated,

"The Hermit's Cell, Feb. 10, 1843.

"O, goddess, for no less you seem, how quickly would I, were the privilege granted me, approach and kiss thy sainted feet! My dear, dear Belinda; when I think of your wonderful powers to bless, I am apt to imagine you as not only superior, in yourself, to the rest of your species, but as belonging to some higher, some more distinguished class of intelligencies. I must confess, my love, that it was no small mortification to me, when I was deprived of your society, by one whom I think you ought not any longer to call by the respectful name of father. I do not attribute anything to your sweet self. Love must succumb, for a time, to authority, but when opportunity offers, it should grasp at freedom, not sink, without an effort, beneath the tumid wave. I extend my hand. Do not disdainfully reject an unworthy, but perhaps not disadvantageous proposal. I never knew what it was to be alone, until I saw and loved, and was forbidden to enjoy the only person for whom I ever had feelings of complete cognation. Since that time my house, occupied by a half-a-dozen beings, not so much unlovely as unloved, has been to me as solitary as a hermitage. And must I spend the remnant of my days, Belinda, in this hermitical manner? If you will only agree to become my wife, I will leave for ever the woman who calls me husband, and the brats which she has taught to call me father, and under Liberty's striped and constellated flag, where Ham's dark sons are taught their proper station, we'll find a happier home than this. Let no scruples prevent you, my dear, from complying. Write soon.

"Yours in haste, in heart, in love, in duty,

"Bickerstaff."

"Miss Belinda Howard."

This elicited no reply. Belinda thought herself not yet reduced to so pitiable a pass as to make an elopement with the renegado eligible. Besides, she knew from her own experience, that one desertion only makes apostacy more easy, and that, as revolution is a very common thing, though *powers to bless* were now acceded to her, the time might come when a reverse would take place; the character of supplicant belong to her; and all her prayers be, by the base bandying Bickerstaff, unheeded. The letter was filed and forgotten. Belinda did not think proper to let Theodore see it. He was as nearly non compos mentis as could be desired. His brain was at as high a degree of temperature as it would be safely heated to, and the art of the *professor* was called into requisition, to keep it from rising or falling. It was a case involving all the consequences of life and death. Miss Howard's knowledge of human nature, however, rendered her fully equal to the important task.

I hope that if a person ever happens to read the story of "Belinda," he will not think me endeavoring to impose upon his credulity, if I insert a correct transcript of the shepherd's last epistle, received by Belinda so late as the 21st of the eventful month. His splendid and pleasantly situated mansion, in the midst of a densely populated tract of country, he again styles dreary and desolate, and dates his letter as before, from

"The Hermit's Cell, Feb. 20th.

"My Dear Belinda — Without a figure I admit your exquisite beauty — in plain language, I love you dearly. My aversion to Josephine becomes daily more confirmed and settled. I dislike every thing she does. I used to think her — whatever else she might be — a proficient in the culinary art, and able, at least, to act well the housewife's part in the kitchen; but now she can prepare nothing for the table that will suit my palate. She perceives this, and racks her invention to overcome my disgust; but she might as well attempt to make her heart congenial to mine. My stomach is nauseated at the very sight of the finest dishes she can order, while the coarsest rusk, or sea-biscuit, if your delicate hand should touch it, would be sweeter than the apples of paradise. Josephine has abated nothing of her attention to me; indeed, it seems to increase in the same ratio as my neglect; but she must not think, thereby, to regain my eternally alienated love. It has gone over to you. I am tired of the fond manner in which she clings to me. I repudiate her, and all her cerimonious regards. I hate her quaint performances of duty. I hate her very kindnesses. You are more of a latitudinarian. I love your liberal Mind — I love your freedom from restraint. I love yourself, Belinda.

"No answer, to my proposal of a closer relationship, has yet been received. I know you are not blameable for this. It is to be imputed to the malignity of your brother — and to that blustering dotard, your father. What right have they to guard you like a child; to imprison you like the commonest culprit. Is love to be enclosed with a wooden fence? No, Belinda. I have devised a scheme for your release, by which you may escape the machinations of them who bear you, as they do me, nothing but ill-will. Clandestine marriage, and nocturnal flight, have been fully prepared for, and you have only to throw yourself into my arms, tell me that I'm loved, and consent to share my fortune; and St. Lawrence will be placed between us and our enemies. My house and lands, in this country, a sufficient support, shall be left to Josephine and *her* fry, so that the world, always severe in judgment, shall not be able to find a bill of indictment against me upon any charge whatever.

"Now, my dear, my adored Belinda, we have but to agree upon the time. I propose to-morrow night. Write me if possible, before that. If not, my carriage will be at the wicket, on the eastern side of the yard of the Clifton Hall, at half past ten precisely.

"Your eternal lover,
"Bickerstaff."

"Miss Belinda Howard."

Who can consider such proceedings as these, and not feel an inclination to disown his species? Why, I had rather have a baboon for my brother, than to confess myself akin to such a reprobate. There is nothing so sacred as not to become the object of mimickry by man. I will leave it to the honesty of church-goers, if "Good Lord deliver us," has not ceased to be a prayer — if genuflection is any longer the sign of humble adoration — if bowing at the *name* of "Jesus," is always a sure indication of confession from the heart? Are words, (answer ye who best can tell,) in any collocation whatever, invariably the vehicles of love, law, or liberty?

"Poor Josephine," said Belinda, as she read this astounding letter, "from my heart I pity you, but you need not fear the loss, through me, of what is scarcely worth retaining. Bickerstaff, you are the object of my perfect scorn! How contemptible is your blandishment, and displaced courtship! How despicable to me appears the man who can disparage his own faithful wife, to gain another and *hate her for her very kindnesses!* This is too much. I never was so insulted in my life. Stand at the gate to-night, and cool the fever of your unlawful love with wintry blasts. To-morrow I shall be the wife of Theodore. Oh, fate, what is my doom? Oh, heaven, protect me!"

"If 'twere well 'twere done, 'twere well
'twere done quickly."

The twenty-second had arrived. Never did a fairer day dawn upon our fair world since Adam and his fair wife, arm in arm, passed the gate of their fair garden. The earth was covered with an even coat of undrifting snow; the trees were ornamented with icicles of every variety of shape and size, and the sun's oblique rays were playing fantasically over Nature's silver mantle.

The music of bells filled the lucid air — Theodore had made his appearance, and a numerous company was collected. He took Belinda by the hand, and, trembling for fear that Bickerstaff might have gained some one among the guests to put in an allegation against her, they stood upon the floor. The minister said — "I require and charge you both, as ye will answer," Etc. Neither of the parties, nor any other person present, knowing any impediment, nor thinking that they would be "coupled together otherwise than God's word doth allow," the ceremony proceeded. To very close questions, each answered, "I will." Theodore gave his "troth," and Belinda pledged her fidelity! He slipped a ring, which looked like gold, upon her fourth finger, and when he said, "I thee worship," he told a solemn truth. There appears to be some deeper meaning, stronger virtue, and greater *adhesive* powers in the use of the ring, than some people are apt to image. "It is nothing but superstition," say they. Well, what of that? That only proves its utility. Superstition always has more effect upon the mind than the belief of truth. I never heard the thing explained by those who know its signification, but perhaps the purity of the *material* might mean that pure love existed between the two; that they had united from pure motives; and that they should enjoy pure pleasure together. It might mean, also, that the commixture formed by blending two into one, when both were pure, was not an alloy, but that the compound was pure also. — The meaning of its *shape* was more obvious. The ring, being a thing *without an end*, might import that the union now perfected, should likewise have no termination.

Theodore and Belinda were "pronounced man and wife together" — a hundred true-hearted friends rushed forward to taste the fair cheek of the blushing bride, and compliments and wishes for prosperity, were poured from every tongue. The rest remains to be told.

The next day after the wedding, Belinda took possession of her new home in the manor house. Duty now concurred with inclination to induce Theodore to make her as happy as she had him, and he flattered himself that this object was fully accomplished, when every thing about the house, or in it, was convenient and comfortable; himself devoted, and all calumnious reports disproved. But, although they were now so inseparably connected; so closely, so mysteriously and divinely joined together, yet he was mistaken in her feelings — she had the heart-ache! Their house, however, though the abode of two kinds of love — love concentrated and love with latitude — was to Theodore a fair representation of the place where there is fullness of joy; while the opposite, or the habitation where hate and harpies rule, is the very domain of Lucifer — only minus the fire.

It will be said, perhaps, that I, who have never passed the ordeal of matrimony myself, have no claim to notice when I speak of its attendant happiness, or misery. I am not particular about attentions, nor writing for the purpose of making court to sex or sectary; and shall, therefore, act with perfect liberty of conduct and of conscience. I love, as well as hate.

The best gift of heaven is sometimes worthy of more praise than poetry can give her; and sometimes I would rather hear the barkings of Cerberus, with all his mouths at once, than the clamors of her tongue. A peaceable, good-natured and intelligent woman, is to be loved and admired; the scold (deliver us!) is to be avoided as the pestilence. But the tempers of Theodore and Belinda were in no way incompatible, and joys succeeded each other in regular succession, like the return of day and night.

CHAPTER IX.

Those who have read this far, and think that a more improbable story than has yet been told cannot possibly be true, had better not look at this chapter at all, though I have good authority for saying that the actual circumstances were very nearly as here related.

Six christian sabbaths had been in a christian manner spent, and the envied and to-be-envied pair were sitting by their own bright fireside, talking of the past — the opposition they had encountered from invidious enemies and mistaken friends, — and how evident it was that *the hand which wheels the silent spheres* had conducted them through the labyrinth of youthful courtship, — where impressions are so easily made and more easily obliterated — into a broad, open, plain road, to harmonize and coalesce together. Theodore thought that Juliet, particularly, must be ashamed of her impotent interference, when old Time, who was now speaking, had finished his tale. "I went to Chatham, a few days before our wedding, on purpose to give her an opportunity of witnessing the ceremony; but she stopped her ears to every thing like reason, and declared, almost with an oath, that she would never, while her life and senses lasted, be for a moment sheltered by the same roof with yourself. Juliet used to love you, Belinda, but, through the malevolence of those who, having no character of their own to lose, make it the business of their lives to destroy that of others, her love is changed to an irreconcileable hatred. But, for myself, were I condemned to death, and offered life upon the hard condition that I should even become indifferent towards you, I would reject the boon with proud disdain, and unbidden, lay my head upon the block."

Belinda fetched a deep sigh when she thought of *old Time finishing his tale!* She appeared contemplative and melancholy — complained of indisposition — and retired, requesting her husband (that he might not be disturbed) to occupy another room from the one in which her bed was placed, and hoping he would give himself no uneasiness, nor be at all alarmed about the restoration of her health.

Theodore was full of inquietude, and, unable to rest, informed his mother of what had happened. She advised him to call a physician. This, although violently opposed by Belinda, who wished to be left entirely alone, was accordingly done with all haste. The doctor had not been many minutes with his patient, when Theodore took him aside and wished him candidly and seriously to give his opinion whether or not the disease would terminate fatally. At this he only laughed, and said, "I think the symptoms, at present, more the sign of life than death. Instead of a coffin, you may procure a cradle — and, instead of powerful medicines, which undermine the constitution and rack the frame, a little *panado*, and perhaps a little *pap*, might be prepared!"

"You're a confounded fool," cried Theodore; "a disgrace to the honorable faculty to which you belong, and unworthy to associate with any set of men of common sense or common decency."

"There is more cause for pleasantry than anger," continues the facetious doctor; "more reason for joy than grief. But you have studied late enough tonight. You must not take in knowledge too rapidly. Get you to bed and put yourself into the skilful hands of nature's sweet restorer. I perceive some symptoms of distemperature. Your eyes have an unusual glare. Your lucubrations are too long continued. Get you to bed and learn the rest to-morrow. You shall then have perfect liberty to ridicule me for my hallucinations, and call me a wiseacre."

Theodore allowed himself to be for once controlled, but not convinced. Like Thomas, he refused to take any thing for granted upon the testimony of others. "I will not believe," said he, and withdrew. But sleep forsook his pillow. This was, he thought, a confirmation of his hopes; "for Solomon says, 'A virtuous woman is a crown to her husband,' and Shakspeare adds, 'Uneasy lies the head that wears a crown.' My head lies uneasy — *ergo*, I wear a crown; but that crown is Belinda — *ergo*, Belinda is a virtuous woman."

Early in the morning, *the tenth of April*, Theodore was roused by Bridget, Belinda's maid, with "very, very happy news. You have a son!" said she, "as fair a child as ever drew a breath! A bright and beautiful boy. Come down and see yourself in miniature, a true representation, a pretty, very pretty picture!" The confident Unwin, like that thunderer, Demosthenes, when Harpalus' golden cup had been accepted, was dumb at last, and, putting his hand to his mouth, motioned the merciless Bridget to stop her prate, and leave him to perform his morning prayers, and *meditations*. I shall not disturb him either, nor obtrude any remarks upon the deep recess of thought; but let him alone in his pensiveness, and hasten to a close.

Belinda had sent for her mother, not, however, letting her know that she was a *grandmother*, and early in the day, her parents both called at the manor house. What could equal their astonishment, when, upon coming into the room, to which they had been conducted by the old lady, Mrs. Unwin, they found the faithful Bridget alone at the bed, and on it, all pale, their own daughter, with little Ichabod by her side! Esq. Howard turned from the sight in disgust, and left the house, without speaking a word. Belinda was touched to the heart. She wished to say something in defence of her situation, to ask her mother's forgiveness and blessing, but her sobs prevented the giving of expression to her emotions. Mrs. Howard stopped but a few minutes, and followed her husband out, not so much as saying when, or if ever, she would call again. Theodore had not yet made his appearance, and the unfortunate Belinda keenly felt all the horrors of her condition. She was admired once and loved, but now, oh! how fallen! how degraded! deserted by her last friend, and set up as a laughing-stock for the derision of the world! Deservedly! "O, that is the unkindliest stab of all."

Moved with pity by the anxiousness and depression of poor Belinda, Mrs. Unwin, the next day, told her not to let her mind be troubled, that she should want for nothing while unable to help herself, or to procure other assistance; but whenever this should be the case, to renounce forever the thoughts of being regarded as any thing but what she was. Theodore, also, was at last so far subdued, by the continued entreaties of his wife, made known to him by the tender hearted Bridget, as to consent to see her — intending, at the same time, to give a long farewell to lover and to love. He was just recovering from a very severe attack of a sort of mania, and was advised that there would be great danger of a relapse, if he thus exposed himself to the contagion. But this was mockery too trifling to notice. He ventured forward, took Belinda by the hand, and, when she said, in a plaintive tone, "My dear, dear husband, forgive me! I deserve more than you can inflict, but, as you hope for heaven, O forgive me! I cannot live unless my mind find peace, and the thoughts of having injured you, is its heaviest load."

"You are forgiven, I love you still," said Theodore, as he carefully conned over the features of Ichabod, in whose face (it was enough!) he traced a resemblance of its mother, "I hope we shall yet, in mutual love, enjoy many happy days together."

Belinda soon became more cheerful, being particularly gratified with the kind attention of her husband, and by perceiving that he had already inbibed a strong attachment for her dear little Ichabod. A week passed pleasantly off, and Belinda began to wonder why no one from the Clifton Hall appeared — not even her mother. Upon being informed that, when last at the manor house, her father had signified his determination "never again so much as to bend his eyes upon so vile a creature, though she might pass him in the street," and that even her mother's words were rather condemnatory than pathetic, she swooned away in her arm-chair.

From that moment she declined rapidly. Her disease was one which no drug could reach. Her mind was convulsed with tormenting thoughts of what she had brought upon herself and connexions; and the mind exceeds the body in its susceptibility of suffering, as well as in the duration of its existence. It reacted with alarming effect upon her tender frame, and another week reduced her to a point which hope itself could scarcely penetrate. She had seen her father's carriage pass and repass, without so much as an inquiry being made whether she was dead or alive. Both Brock and Mrs. Newton, (formerly Miss Sophia Howard,) had contemptuously refused to accept the warmest invitations to visit her; and her repenting with desperation, like a worm in a bud, was fast eating out the very core of life.

Theodore, about this time, received a note from Bickerstaff, to this effect, that, as a late event had vindicated his truth and *honor*, he hoped they should not be able to make up all differences; reconcile whatever had appeared inconsistent, and re-establish a friendly communication. Saying, at the same time that as he did not think himself "worse than an infidel," he would not refuse to "provide for those of *his own* household!" This may be called the acme of impudence.

Word being accidentally carried to the Clifton Hall that Belinda was fast wasting away by a malady which had baffled the profound skill of a kind physician — but that she could not die in peace without acknowledging her faults and being forgiven, to and by both earth and heaven — all the tender feelings of parents, brothers and sisters, returned to the bosoms of her seemingly heartless friends. They were soon standing at her bed-side, and listening to the most frightful confession, delivered in the most thrilling accents, that ever reached the ears of human beings.

She dated her misfortunes back to the time of Barnabas and Fitz Rowland. On the *fifth of June*, 1833, she believed her fate to have been forever sealed. That was her last opportunity of saving herself from disgrace and ruin; and, with her eyes open — not blinded by destiny — she had neglected to take that favorable tide at the ebb. The anniversary of that day had ever since been marked by some unfortunate event! "But, what drives me," said she, "entirely to despair, are the thoughts of my having so often insulted the Judge of all the earth to his face, by pretending to worship, (that I might be seen of men,) while with my heart his name was many times blasphemed. Now, also, my prayers are unheeded, and my calamities derided." Her words — her voice — her looks, conveyed horror to the souls of those who heard her speak, and saw her visage wild and wretched. To see a beautiful and accomplished lady — one who, by a different course of conduct, might have been an honor to her family and a blessing to her species, lying in this wretched state, is more calculated to strike the mind with awe, than the sight of Moscow in its ruins. I am not more easily startled than most other persons. I am pleased with a view of the grand and wonderful in nature. I love to see the clouds lift o'er the hills their crested heads in majesty sublime, and, with bold front, advance in solid phalanx. I love to see the forked lightnings fly abroad, like angels sent upon some important message, and hear them speak with a voice like Him who called creation into being. I have been tossed, without distraction, over stormy, foaming billows, while the frail bark visited, in quick succession, the upper and the lower regions. I once stood in a horrid amphitheatre, upon a slippery and well-washed pavement — behind my back a lofty and jutty wall arose, built by the hand which built the world, and o'er my head, Niagara, in terrible confusion, tumbled. That is the place to which chaos and old night retired when driven from their universal dominion by the words, "Let there be light." There, where mighty turbulence is bound in adamant, I stood perfectly composed and admired the furious commotion; but the unhappy death-bed, I will confess, affected me with sensations, not only of sympathy, but of indescribable terror. It is easy to tell what it is not — but what is it? That question must remain unanswered. It beggars all description.

"I have brought shame, ignominy, and disgrace upon you all," said Belinda, always eloquent, "and *eternal ruin* upon myself. He who shakes the nations with a stamp, and could annihilate the world with a frown, is angry with me, and I dare not look towards heaven, nor think of mercy. I have been the bane of you all, and you will not forgive me."

Her friends assured her that she was most cordially forgiven by them, and prayed that the pardon might be as freely granted, through the infinite merits of the Redeemer. A ray of hope beamed through the thick shades of despair. Her prayers now showed that "tired dissimulation had dropped its mask." Her prospects brightened. Her countenance took a different expression. A smile passed across her face. Her forebodings of a speedy condemnation were succeeded by a confident expectation of being welcomed to the realms of bliss immediately upon her dissolution, which she knew was approaching. Had Hume or Bolingbroke been there, he would have been convinced of the existence of a Mediator. Had Gregory XVI, been there, he would have been satisfied that mercy *may* be obtained without his intervention. Had all the world been witnesses of the scene, — why, there had been none left to doubt the impartiality of heaven, or the truths of a revealed religion, untrammeled by the inextricable windings of explainers and interpretors. The grisly terror, death, continued his advances, with furious and frequent onsets, driving trembling life with precipitation from post to post; a wall was carried and a tower fell, but the soul looked calmly on, and fearlessly beheld the destruction of its shattered tenement. The conduct of Theodore evidenced the genuineness of his affection for his wife. A favorable symptom elated his spirits, quickened his motions, and gave lustre to his eye; a relapse cast a gloom over his mind, weakened his very nerves, and streaked his manly cheek with tears. He scarcely allowed himself an hour's repose, but watched with intense feeling, for fear the fluttering spirit should escape, and he not have an opportunity of closing her eyes. For several days Belinda had now been resigned to her fate — she even triumphed in the thoughts of death, and wished the minutes shorter. She warned them about her against running the desperate risk which she had — and by which her all, of sublunary things, was lost, and her *crown* so imminently endangered. She deliberately and cheerfully presented different articles of dress, books, and furniture, to Brock and Mrs. Newton — to her parents and beloved husband. Ichabod was accepted by her mother-in-law. She begged her father to allow her a very small piece of land in the corner of a certain field, for a solitary grave. Her body, she said, was unworthy to lie in the church-yard, as much so as that of any other person who had by any other means, committed suicide. Every thing being settled agreeably to her wishes, she composed herself to sleep. That sleep was an everlasting sleep! A smile still trembling on her lips, but her eye had lost its brilliancy; her heart, at last, had ceased its palpitations, and the spark of life slowly, softly, sweetly settling down, had touched the wave, and was forever extinguished. In silent grief, Theodore sat motionless. Of the numbers who witnessed the blissful exit, he was perhaps the only one that felt pure, unmingled sorrow. Mrs. Howard said she did not wish Belinda back — others expressed a hope that their own end might be equally happy, and all agreed, that *without controversy*, her life had been a tissue of contrarieties, and her death a very *great mystery*.

Three days were allowed for the preparations for the funeral; during which time the manor house was crowded with visitors, anxious to see once more the face of her whom all either envied, pitied, or admired. A general feeling of melancholy and dejection seemed to pervade all classes of the community, as if some patriot hero, the pillar and support of his country, had fallen. The hour for the last sad service had come. The corpse was placed within a splendid covered coffin, with the initials B.U., in gilt, upon each side of it, and carried on men's shoulders to the grave. The concourse of people was immense, forming a procession extending nearly a mile. Of all those who had ever heard the name of Belinda, Bickerstaff and McLeod were almost the only persons that were not found in the company. They stood *afar off*, like the ships at the burning of Babylon, and cried, saying, "Alas! alas! for all our hopes are *come to nought!*" Like a black cloud hovering over the place where the earth has opened its monstrous jaws and swallowed, at a gulp, some fated city down, the mournfully moving multitude at last stood still upon a beautiful grass plat, at the farthest edge of Esquire Howard's estate. An oblong, at a distance from the din of busy life, and of dimensions small, was prepared to receive the pride of this world. At the head of her whose love death

121

itself could not subdue or terminate, stood Theodore like a tombstone, straight and pallid, and, in his face, quite legibly were stamped the lines of grief. And, when the coffin slowly lowered from the sight, and with it prematurely blasted hopes; and when the cords dragged dolefully from underneath; and when the first cold clods above the vault played rumbling, mournful music to the ear, many a sigh escaped, and a gentle shower of crystal drops from many hundred eyes, bedewed the unconscious earth.